A Crabby Killer

A Mooseamuck Island Cozy Mystery

Leighann Dobbs

A Crabby Killer
Copyright © 2015 Leighann Dobbs
http://www.leighanndobbs.com
Cover art by: http://www.tina-adams.com/design

All Rights Reserved.

This is a work of fiction. None of it is real. All names, places, and events are products of the author's imagination. Any resemblance to real names, places, or events are purely coincidental, and should not be construed as being real.

No part of this work may be used or reproduced in any manner, except as allowable under "fair use," without the express written permission of the author.

Also by Leighann Dobbs

KATE DIAMOND
Adventure/Suspense Series

Hidden Agemda
Ancient Hiss Story

MYSTIC NOTCH
Cats & Magic Cozy Mystery Series

Ghostly Paws
A Spirited Tail
A Mew To A Kill

BLACKMOORE SISTERS
Cozy Mystery Series

Dead Wrong
Dead & Buried
Dead Tide
Buried Secrets
Deadly Intentions
A Grave Mistake

MOOSEAMUCK ISLAND
Cozy Mystery Series

A Zen For Murder

LEXY BAKER
Cozy Mystery Series

Lexy Baker Cozy Mystery Series
Boxed Set Vol 1 (Books 1-4)

Or buy the books separately:

Killer Cupcakes (Book 1)
Dying For Danish (Book 2)
Murder, Money and Marzipan (Book 3)
3 Bodies and a Biscotti (Book 4)
Brownies, Bodies & Bad Guys (Book 5)
Bake, Battle & Roll (Book 6)
Wedded Blintz (Book 7)
Scones, Skulls & Scams (Book 8)
Ice Cream Murder (Book 9)
Mummified Meringues (Book 10)
Brutal Brulee (Book 11 - Novella)

CONTEMPORARY ROMANCE

Sweet Escapes
Reluctant Romance

A Crabby Killer

Chapter 1

Claire Watkins wrinkled her nose against the stinging assault of chemicals. She slid her eyes toward Mary Lou Prichard, seated in the hairdresser's chair to her left. Mary Lou had her nose buried in the latest issue of *Elle Magazine*, happily oblivious to the fact that whatever treatment was being put on her hair smelled like rotten eggs.

Claire shifted in her seat, pointed her nose away from Mary Lou, and looked out the window at the Crab Cove pier where preparations for the annual Crab Festival were under way. The festival was one of many events that the Mooseamuck Island residents put on to lure tourists to their quaint, New England paradise just off the coast of Maine.

Though most of the locals would have preferred to limit the ferry service in the hope that 'outsiders' never found the island, and to keep the population from tripling in the summer, they also knew that most of their businesses survived on tourist money. So, it was with mixed feelings that they hosted the festivals and events that attracted the tourists.

Various tents and tables were being set up along the waterfront. Tomorrow, Saturday, the festival would be in full swing. The tents would be loaded with vendors, hawking everything from hot dogs to sea glass jewelry. The docks would be crowded with tourists and locals.

But right now, there were only a handful of people setting up, in addition to the fishermen who were normally there. Next to one of the tents, local fisherman and tour boat operator, Donovan Hicks, waved his arms around in a heated conversation with a tall, lanky man that Claire did not recognize. She supposed the man must be a tourist or some sort of vendor. He'd probably tried to talk Donovan down on the price of one of his whale watching tours or fishing cruises and Donovan had taken offense. Donovan could be a little hot-headed.

A short, stout woman walking down the dock with an overloaded tote bag caught Claire's eye. Mae Biddeford. Claire watched as she purposefully clattered down the dock. She turned the corner, almost running into the strange man who had just ended his conversation with Donovan and was staring at the fisherman's back as he stomped off toward the end of the dock where he parked his fleet of tour boats.

Mae stopped short in her tracks. The man turned to face her. From Claire's vantage point inside the beauty parlor across the street, she could see the startled expression on Mae's face. She watched the tote bag slip from

Mae's hand and thud onto the dock. Jars of dark purple jam bounced out and smashed on the wooden boards, leaving a gooey, glass-infused clump.

Claire wondered why Mae had so many jams. She knew Mae traded them for services and goods just like the rest of the longtime residents of Mooseamuck Island who still used the barter system that their grandparents had worked out before them. But with that much jam, Mae must have had one heck of a purchase to make.

On the dock, Mae was engaging in a heated conversation with the tall, lanky man, ignoring the mess at her feet. She waved her arms wildly as she yelled. The man leaned down, getting in her face and yelled back. Claire was too far away to hear what they were saying, but she strained forward in her seat anyway.

What was *that* all about?

Mae was certainly overreacting to the jam-dropping incident. After all, it wasn't even the man's fault that she'd dropped the bag.

Claire's training as a criminal psychologist kicked in as she studied the body language between Mae and the stranger. The fight was about more than some spilled jam, she was sure of it. The way Mae flailed her arms suggested that she was frustrated and angry--much more angry than simply bumping into a stranger warranted. And the man's demeanor seemed almost menacing.

Claire felt a tingling premonition—something wasn't right.

As she watched, Mae wagged her finger in the man's face. He turned and stormed off toward the parking lot leaving Mae on the dock, staring after him with a strangled look on her face.

"You ready?"

"What?" Claire tore her gaze from the window to see her hair stylist, Florence Ryder, standing next to her.

Florence jerked her head toward the sinks in the back. "It's your turn."

"Oh, okay." Claire got up from the chair, the long, black plastic bib swirling around her. Before she disappeared into the back room, she gave one final glance over her shoulder, just in time to see the man pull out of the parking lot and head up Moose Hill Road in a dark blue Mercedes.

***

Dominic Benedetti parked his Smart Car in the scenic overlook and gazed out over the sparkling Atlantic Ocean. He unfolded himself from the car, took a deep breath of the salty sea air, then turned and started walking down Moose Hill Road in concordance with his self-imposed exercise regimen.

Dom had never had to worry about his weight before, but now that he was in his sixties, he was no longer a young man and his fondness for Italian pastry and desserts had caused his pants to tighten. So, he had taken to parking his car at least one mile from his various destinations around town. So far, it was working—he'd managed to rack up quite a few miles on his new Nike sneakers just this week alone.

Today's destination was *Chowders*, a restaurant that catered to the locals and where he was about to test out the diner's version of tiramisu.

He walked with a spring in his step, the corners of his lips tugging as he thought of how his wife used to joke about how thin he was. What would she think now? He was surprised to find that the mere thought of her didn't hurt as much as it used to.

He'd been married to Sophia, the love of his life, for forty-five years. Her cancer diagnosis had destroyed him and when she'd died two years ago, a big part of Dom had died with her. But over time, the knife that pierced and twisted in his heart every time he thought about her had become less painful.

He would have thought that the fact that it didn't twist as deeply now would be good, but it made him feel sad and empty. Grief had rushed in to fill the hole left after her death and now that the grief was receding, what did he have left?

The only thing Dom really had left in his life, besides his daughters who lived far away, was his love of investigating. Formerly a police detective and, in his later years, a police consultant, Dom had been instrumental in solving several high-profile cases in Boston, Massachusetts. He'd been in the papers more than once and he was the closest thing they had to a celebrity on the island.

This celebrity status had gotten him accepted by the islanders, which was quite a feat since the locals on Mooseamuck Island did not readily accept 'outsiders' into their ranks. He had to admit, he'd been flattered and excited when they'd started coming to him to solve various problems.

At first, it had been simple things like finding a lost

set of keys or getting a cat out of a tree, but recently he'd solved the island's first murder case in decades. After several years in retirement, he had to admit that case had bolstered his ego and made him feel useful again. The only fly in the ointment was that he'd had to pair up with Claire Watkins.

Claire was nice enough as a person, but in his heyday down in Boston, Claire had also been a consultant on many of his cases. The department felt her expertise in human behavior would help them analyze the actions of the suspects so they could zero in on the identity of the killer. Claire relied on gut instinct, emotion, and body language—all that touchy-feely stuff that Dom couldn't get on board with.

Dom felt that it was critical to use logic when investigating. He liked to dig out the clues and follow them the old-fashioned way. Dom and Claire had butted heads more than once, but they'd always been professional and cordial. Over the years, they'd solved a lot of cases together and formed a relationship of grudging respect. But Dom still preferred to work alone and do things *his* way.

He remembered his surprise when he'd discovered Claire lived right down the hill from him on the island that Dom had adopted as his home after Sophia's death. On the job, they'd rarely talked about personal matters and he'd had no idea his former antagonistic partner resided here when he'd decided to make the island his new home.

Unbeknownst to him, Claire had grown up on the island and had moved here years earlier to take care of her dying father. That past spring, when murder had visited the island, they were called upon to team up and use their skills to ferret out the killer. It had worked well, and Dom had to admit that the case had done a lot to bolster his ego and alleviate his fears that age had dampened his ability to detect.

Dom might even admit that investigating with Claire had been fun … sometimes. But he still didn't want to team up with her on any future cases, should there even be any.

But today, all he had to look forward to was trying out the dessert that Sarah White, the owner of *Chowders*, had concocted. He had talked her into introducing an Italian menu and had become her unofficial taste-tester. It was an enjoyable job and Dom, with his Italian heritage and love of its food, was perfect for it.

Sarah was a relative newcomer to the island, having bought the diner from its longtime owner a few years back. She'd kept the chef, and the menu hadn't changed too much, which was fine with the clientele who had been frequenting it for generations. It was a little off the beaten path, so not many tourists ever found it and that was fine with the locals—they preferred to keep it to themselves.

Sarah was a few years younger than Dom's youngest daughter, and he had come to think of her as a surrogate daughter. It was probably her sad demeanor that made him feel fatherly. Dom didn't know much about Sarah's personal life before she came to the island, but his investigator's instincts told him that she had a burning secret which she kept close to her vest.

Dom rounded the corner, bringing *Chowders* into view. It was late afternoon, well before the dinner crowd. Dom noticed with satisfaction that the parking lot was empty. He preferred to taste test the desserts without an audience.

His brows tugged together when a dark blue Mercedes pulled in. He watched as a tall, lanky man got out. Probably a tourist, Dom guessed, since he'd never seen him before.

The man went into the diner. Dom was still a good two hundred feet from the building, but he had a clear view through the plate glass window in the front. The man approached the counter behind which Sarah stood. Dom couldn't see perfectly nor could he hear, but by the gestures of their arms, he could have sworn the man and Sarah were having a violent argument.

His gut tightened and he broke into a trot. Was Sarah in trouble?

He was about a hundred feet away when the man slammed the door on his way out of the diner. His face twisted in a viscous snarl, he got into his car and peeled out of the parking lot.

Dom kept up the pace, reaching the diner a few seconds later. "What was that all about?"

Sarah turned to him. "What?"

"That man. It looked like you were arguing."

Sarah avoided eye contact. "No. Not really."

"Then why did he rush off like that? What did he want?"

Sarah shrugged. "He wanted a pizza. We don't make pizza."

Dom stared at her across the counter. She raised her chin and looked him in the eye. Her gaze was steady, but her face was flushed and her hands trembled.

"Are you ready for the tiramisu?" She tried to make her voice sound light, but Dom was not fooled. He knew something was wrong. He could tell she didn't want to talk about it, though, so he let it go.

"Sure." As he took a seat at the counter, his great, bushy eyebrows started to tingle—a sure sign that something was amiss. But he didn't need his eyebrows to tell him the angry stranger had Sarah rattled about something.

There was more to the man's visit than met the eye and Dom didn't think it was anything as benign as wanting a pizza that Sarah couldn't serve.

Chapter 2

Dom slid his fork through the creamy dessert. He brought the generous bite to his mouth and inhaled the tantalizing smell of coffee and chocolate. He nibbled the espresso-infused lady fingers. They were perfect—not too soggy, but not dry, either. He put a dollop of the creamy filling on his tongue. It was sweet and satisfying, but it could use more tang—maybe he should tell Sarah to add a smidge more mascarpone.

Sarah had moved over to the stainless steel table in the middle of the kitchen, leaving Dom seated alone at the counter to perform his taste test. The counter was open to the kitchen and he could see her chopping onions, her blonde hair pulled back into a ponytail that swayed halfway down her back. The rhythmic chop-chop-chop had a meditative effect. Dom closed his eyes and lost himself in the taste of the tiramisu, which triggered memories of the delights that came from his Nonna's kitchen when he was a boy.

He was savoring the final bite when the door whooshed open and Mae Biddeford came in, looking distressed.

His eyes fell on the dark purple-stained tote bag she had clutched against her chest. The chop-chop-chop sounds stopped and Sarah looked up from the cutting board, the line between her brows deepening. "What happened to your bag?"

Mae flushed. "Gosh, I am—"

The door whooshed open again and Claire Watkins came in, her damp, gray hair curling haphazardly around her head.

"Hi." Claire frowned at Mae's bag, and Dom figured Claire was wondering the same thing he and Sarah were about the stain.

"Hi, Claire." Mae followed Claire's gaze to the tote. "I was just about to apologize to Sarah. You see, I was supposed to bring some blackberry jam jars I made special for *Chowders* so Sarah could see if they were something she wanted to put in the diner, but I dropped the jars and they broke." She gave a half-shrug, half-grimace. "I can be so clumsy sometimes."

"Oh, that's okay," Sarah soothed. "You can bring more jars some other time."

"I did manage to salvage some things." Mae rummaged in the bag, pulling out a broken piece of glass and a ball of brown twine which she set on the counter. She pointed to the glass that had a brown paper label with *Chowders* written in white and a light blue starfish above the words 'Blackberry Jam'. "This here is the label and then I wrap the twine around the top of the jar and tie it in a bow. Gives it a nice, homey appearance and the twine is biodegradable."

Sarah studied the two items. "These look great. I can picture what it would look like and I think the jam jars will be wonderful."

A look of relief passed across Mae's face, but Dom had his eye on Claire. He could tell she was assessing the situation more intently than just a casual encounter.

Dom flicked his eyes toward Sarah. She was acting as if everything was fine, but he could still see a slight tremor in her hand. He watched Claire's gaze move from Mae to the piece of glass to Sarah.

Did Claire sense that something was amiss?

Dom wouldn't be surprised if Claire suspected something wasn't right with Sarah. Due to Claire's training, she was a keen observer of people and Dom knew her skills were still sharp, even though she was in her seventies. And the look on her face right now had Dom wondering if Claire knew something about Sarah's argument with the tall, lanky man that Dom didn't.

***

Claire's eyes flicked from Sarah to the dark purple stains on Mae's tote to Mae's face. "That bag must have had a lot of jam in it. What made you drop it?"

Mae flushed. "Well, I guess the bag was a little too heavy for me. I should have realized a bag this size full of glass jam jars would weigh too much. I thought I could carry it all the way here, but it slipped out of my hand."

Mae kept her eyes on the purple stain the whole time she was talking and Claire got the impression she was avoiding eye contact. Claire wondered why Mae was lying. Why didn't she want them to know about the tall, lanky man?

"Anyway," Mae continued, "I got the twine from Bob Cleary. He uses it on the Barnacle Bob's fishing boats. So, I thought it would be cute to put it on the jam jars. You know, tie it all together." They laughed at her little joke. "I've already cut up the rest of the twine into small sections, so if you think these will be okay, I'll go right home and make some more."

"There's no need to rush," Sarah said.

"Oh, no problem. I need to get this done today before the insp— ... err ... before I get busy with my duties on the planning committee." Mae turned to Claire. "Should we meet here early tomorrow morning for breakfast?"

That was a good question. Several of the regulars who usually met for breakfast at *Chowders* were on the planning committee for the Crab Festival. The festival officially opened at nine but they needed to get down to the docks early to make sure everything was in order.

"I think we need to get to the pier by eight, so it might be much too early to have breakfast here. Maybe we should meet at the pier," Claire suggested.

"Right. Of course," Mae nodded. "We could have breakfast here after."

"I'll tell the others." Claire fished her phone out of her pocket.

"Can I get you something while you text them?" Sarah raised her brows at Claire.

"What? Oh …" Claire had forgotten that she hadn't actually come to *Chowders* for anything. She'd been on her way home and had seen Mae going in and followed her. She was hoping to learn about the mysterious man Mae had argued with on the dock, but since Mae clearly didn't want anyone to know about the argument, Claire wasn't going to let the cat out of the bag by asking.

But Claire was used to thinking on her feet, so she blurted out, "I'll have a Greek salad. I forgot to make something for dinner."

"Coming right up." Sarah turned toward the back and started preparing the salad.

"I guess I'll be going. Gotta work on that jam." Mae bustled out the door, leaving Claire and Dom in the front of the diner while Sarah worked on the salad in the back.

"What have you got there?" Claire nodded toward Dom's plate, which now held only a few crumbs and a smudge of creamy filling.

Dom smiled. "I'm testing out Sarah's rendition of tiramisu."

Claire raised her brows. "Any good?"

"Most definitely. Maybe it could use a little more mascarpone, though." Dom slid his eyes over toward Sarah, who smiled and nodded.

Sarah brought the salad over in a to-go bag. As Claire paid for it, she got the feeling that Dom was watching her rather intently.

"Well, I'll be on my way." Claire nodded at Sarah, then Dom.

She briefly entertained the idea of asking them if either of them thought Mae's story of dropping the jam was odd. She had the distinct impression something was 'off' in the diner, and she wondered if it had anything to do with Mae's argument with the tall, lanky stranger.

As she turned toward the door, she saw Dom reach up and smooth out one of his eyebrows. The gesture gave Claire pause. After working with him all those years, she'd become very familiar with his gestures.

She was trained to notice people's body language—their 'tells', as she called them—and interpret their meaning. And Dom preening his brows could mean only one thing—he knew something was going on … and it looked like he had no intention of cluing her in.

Chapter 3

Claire woke up the next day to clear, blue skies. She stretched and climbed out of bed, thankful that she didn't suffer from the aches and pains that many her age complained about. She attributed that to her strict health regimen and hurried downstairs where she measured out a tablespoon of apple cider vinegar and squeezed half a lemon into heated, purified water.

From her kitchen window up high on Israel Head Hill, she had a stunning, bird's-eye-view of the Atlantic Ocean. The view drew her outside and she took her steaming mug into the large garden that encompassed the east side of the old, stone cottage in which she lived.

The cottage had been her parents' house, the one she'd grown up in. She'd been raised on the island, then gone off to college in Boston and ended up spending most of her adult life down there. When her father took ill, she'd come back to Mooseamuck Island to care for him and, realizing this was her true home, had never left.

The garden had been her mother's pride and joy. She'd designed the layout and planted the flowers. Her father had built the planters, installed the stone benches and made the sturdy fence at the east edge of the yard that kept one from falling down the steep cliff onto the scenic road that wound around directly below. Claire had spent the last two years restoring the garden, which had fallen into disrepair.

Claire perched on one of the stone benches, her lips puckering and her face scrunching up as she sipped her acidic elixir. Drinking the apple cider vinegar and lemon juice tea was an acquired taste and, after two years, Claire still hadn't quite acquired it but the vile taste was a small price to pay for good health.

Claire tried to take her mind off the drink by focusing on the gorgeous view while the sun warmed her face. It was early morning and the strength of the sun promised a hot day—perfect for the Crab Festival. Claire shifted her view from the expansive sea of cobalt blue waves to the left where she could just see the edge of Crab Cove and a small section of the pier.

The view reminded her of the jam incident she'd witnessed the day before.

Who was the mysterious man?

Was Mae in some kind of trouble?

And what did Dom know about it?

None of it made any sense. If something was going on, surely she would have heard. But Dom had been preening his eyebrow—didn't that mean something? Then again, maybe he just had an itch.

"Meow."

Claire smiled at the fluffy Maine Coon she called Porch Cat as it wound its way through her garden. Claire didn't know much about that cat, though she thought Mae had told her once the big cat was a 'him'. All she knew was that he frequently showed up on the porches, decks and driveways of many of the homes in the area—thus the nickname 'Porch Cat'.

Claire didn't know if he had a home, but he looked to be well-fed and well-groomed. Of course, that didn't stop her from putting the occasional plate of food out, just in case.

Claire reached down to pet him and was rewarded with a loud purr. The cat twitched his bushy tail several times, then wandered off toward a row of white impatiens. Porch Cat rubbed against the plant and a dead flower dropped to the ground, reminding Claire she needed to do some pruning and dead-heading.

She followed Porch Cat through a path of impatiens, petunias and geraniums, picking off dead leaves and flowers as they went. When they got to the fence at the edge of the yard, Porch Cat poked his head under the lowest railing and looked down at Crab Cove.

"Meow!"

Claire followed the cat's gaze. Down below, she could make out the very edge of the pier where the activity was starting. "Yes, Porch Cat. There's a festival in town today. Are you going?"

"Meow!"

"Oh, sure, there will be lots of crabs and fish for you to eat."

Claire was too far up to see much of what was going on, but the activity told her she had better get a move-on and get down there to inspect the setup. So far, it was just the vendors on the pier. The festival didn't start for another hour and a half. The parking lot was pretty much empty as the locals had all parked in back of the stores that lined the street across from the water so as to leave ample easy parking for money-paying tourists in the main lot.

Of course, there were a few locals who insisted on taking up a spot in the pier parking lot. Claire's lips pursed as she noticed Brad Wellington's station wagon and Mary O'Brien's Toyota right in the front row. Those two always thought the rules didn't apply to them.

Claire was thinking about whether or not she could have her nephew, Robby, the chief of police, give them some sort of ticket when another car caught her eye, one she was sure shouldn't be there—a dark blue Mercedes.

***

Claire parked her old, brown Fiat behind the hair salon and crossed the street to the pier, glancing over at the blue Mercedes and then craning her neck to see if she could spot the tall, lanky man. She couldn't.

The festival tents were set up in a row down the pier's length and the rest of the committee was already standing at the entrance in a tight knot. Dom stood off to one side, next to Claire's best friend and island postmistress,

Jane Kuhn. Beside Jane stood Norma Hopper, the island's resident artist and next to her was Tom Landry ,whose family farm abutted Mae Biddeford's—who, Claire noticed, was strangely absent.

"About time you got here." Norma scowled at Claire from under her wide-brimmed hat. Claire wasn't offended by Norma's brusque manner. The attitude was typical for the elderly artist and Claire knew her bark was worse than her bite.

"Have you been waiting long?" Claire asked.

"No." Jane glared at Norma. "Norma is just being impatient."

"Well, I don't have all day to sit around doing nothing. I'm not retired like you folks. I work for a living in order to pay the rent." Norma thumped her cane on the wooden planks. "So if everyone is here, then let's get a move on."

Claire twisted around, squinting down the road to see if a car was coming. "Mae isn't here yet. Should we wait for her?"

Dom made a show of looking at his watch. "It's eight ten. I don't think we have time to wait. Let's start our inspection and she can jump in when she comes down."

The dark purple stain on the dock that ran at a right angle to the pier they were standing on caught Claire's eye and her stomach roiled uneasily. "Okay. I guess that makes sense."

They proceeded down the pier. Their job was to make sure the tents were set up properly and there were no safety issues, such as tent poles or ties people could trip over, as well as make sure the tents with food had adequate refrigeration and storage facilities and food wasn't left out in the open to spoil in the August heat.

The sun grew hotter as they walked along their inspection route. The seagulls must have sensed the opportunity for stealing food and they flocked around, perching on the pylons at the end of the docks that stretched out from the main pier. Their cries echoed across the water.

Tom carried the clipboard with their 'punch list'. In each tent, he went through the list of items they were tasked to inspect. Norma made sarcastic remarks. Jane tempered Norma's remarks by saying something positive about each vendor's display. Dom took it all in with watchful eyes and thoughtful silence.

Claire kept her eyes peeled for the tall, lanky man. She figured he must be setting up in one of the tents. Was he a vendor? Most likely. Maybe he was up to something shady and that's why he and Mae were fighting. If he was up to something, the committee might discover it. Claire wondered what they should do if they did discover it—no one had told them how far they should go to wield their power and she began to worry about just how much authority they had, if any.

Luckily, no wielding of power was necessary. Claire wasn't actually sure what they were supposed to do in the event they found an 'infraction', but all the tents were set up properly, so she needn't have worried.

She enjoyed getting a preview of what was going to be in the festival. She made a mental note of some of the booths she planned on returning to, like the Dunbartons' local honey stand and Ina's tie-dyed scarfs. She also wanted to check out the tent that had some fantastic-looking cookies from the new bakery in town. She never saw the tall, lanky man.

At the end of the line was the main attraction—the big crab boil. Crab Cove didn't get its name by accident. The cove was loaded with several varieties of ocean crabs. People came to the island specifically to taste the crab salad, crab legs, crab dinners, crab rolls and stuffed crab. The islanders had found a way to capitalize on that by having the largest crab boil on the East Coast and tourists came to see and taste it.

The 'largest' crab boil included a gigantic, cast iron pot which must have been about five feet across.

Claire had no idea where they'd even acquired such a pot. The darn thing took ten men to carry to the fire pit that had been dug in the grassy section of land next to the very end of the pier. Right now, the pot sat atop stacks of wood, which would be lit on fire to create the boil. Claire shuddered to think of how many crabs would give their lives to provide the festival-goers with a tasty lunch.

Norma scowled at the pot, whose lid was tilted up an inch on the right instead of sitting level in the grooves. "Idiots don't even know how to put the cover on right."

"Wait a minute." Dom stepped closer to the side of the pot, his boots scuffing the two-foot dirt ring that surrounded the fire pit. "That must mean there's something in it."

"I thought they didn't put the crabs in until noon," Jane said.

"That's right," Norma huffed. "And it's up to us to

make sure this pot is clean which it looks to me like it might not be." She whipped her cane up and hooked it under the lid, then tugged with a strength that should have been impossible for a bent-over lady of her age. The lid slid aside about six inches.

They all stepped forward and looked into the pot.

Claire felt the blood rush to her head. Her wide eyes battled with her brain, which refused to believe what they saw inside.

The clipboard slipped from Tom's hand and clattered on the ground.

The gull's cries faded away and then disappeared altogether, drowned out by the screams of Jane who was standing beside her.

Inside the pot was the tall, lanky man who drove the blue Mercedes, and he was undoubtedly dead.

Chapter 4

"Who the heck is that?" Norma demanded after Jane stopped screaming.

Claire was wondering the same thing. She glanced over at Dom and caught him looking at her out of the corner of his eye. Did he think *she* knew who the man was? Maybe *he* knew and was looking to see if she recognized the body.

Apparently, Jane's screams had summoned everyone within hearing distance and before anyone could answer Norma's question, a crowd was rushing down the pier toward them.

Dom turned around, holding his hands up to stop them from coming onto the dirt area. "Don't come any further. This is a crime scene now." Dom turned back to face Claire and the others. "Let's try to get onto the pier without disturbing too much."

Dom was right. Claire looked down. There could be footprints or other evidence in the dirt and they'd just trampled most of it. Tom gingerly picked up the clipboard and they all tip-toed onto the wooden boards of the pier.

"Yoo hoo! Sorry I'm late." Claire whipped around to see Mae bustling down the pier. She stopped short about ten feet from them. "What?"

Tom stepped toward Mae. "We've had a little incident," he said soothingly.

Claire caught the look of surprise on Mae's face at Tom's gentle tone. But Claire was not surprised. Tom and Mae lived on abutting farms that their families had owned for generations. Tom's was a goat and dairy farm and Mae's was a fruit farm. The two families had had an ongoing feud since Tom and Mae had been in kindergarten. No one remembered what the feud was about, but that didn't stop them from acting antagonisticly toward each other.

Claire suspected the reason for the way they acted had less to do with the feud and more to do with their inner feelings. Feelings that maybe the two of them didn't care to admit they had because they were too invested in their family feud.

Mae scowled at Tom. "What do you mean an 'incident'? I wasn't that late."

"It's not about you being late," Jane cut in. She took a deep breath and Claire figured she was trying to find the words to tell Mae about their discovery.

"Oh, for crying out loud, just tell her. She's a big girl," Norma huffed at Jane, then turned to Mae. "We found a body in the crab kettle."

Mae gasped. "A body? You mean a dead person?"

Norma rolled her eyes. "Yes. A dead person. And I'd still like to know who it is."

Claire noticed Dom preening his brows while he watched Mae's reaction. Did he know something about Mae and the dead man? Surely he didn't suspect her of killing the guy. How would she get him in the pot? And she looked so surprised that Claire was sure she didn't already know a body was in there.

No one killed someone over spilled jam and besides, if Mae had killed him, she wouldn't just come sauntering down the pier toward them—and the body—would she? Claire's mind flashed on some of her old cases where that was exactly what the killer had done—blend into the crowd of on-lookers because it was the last thing the investigator would expect.

"Step aside." Claire's nephew and Mooseamuck Island chief of police, Robby Skinner, pushed his way through the gathering crowd. "Whats going on?"

Claire pointed to the kettle and he stepped over and looked in, his face sagging. "Oh, no, not another one."

Claire grimaced. Mooseamuck Island hadn't had a murder in over a hundred years, and now there had been two in one year ... and the year wasn't even over yet.

"What do you know about this?" Robby looked at her.

"What do you mean? Why would I know anything?" Claire said defensively.

"Well you *are* here …"

Claire sighed. "I don't know anything about it. I'm

here because I'm on the festival committee and we were down here doing our inspection when we found him like that."

"Was he boiled?" Norma cut in.

Robby peered into the pot again. "I don't think so. There's no water and he doesn't look ... um ... cooked."

"Yech," the crowd said.

"Okay, I need you all to stay where you are," Robby commanded. "I'm going to have to call the mainland and get a homicide detective over here."

Claire's heart pinched at the look on Robby's face. His experience with homicide investigation was limited to the one murder they'd had several months earlier. He'd done a good job then, but he still wasn't trained in homicide detecting.

Claire could tell he wanted to be in charge, but murder was serious business and Robby knew they needed an experienced detective. Hopefully, the one they sent from the mainland would give Robby leeway to do a lot of the work ... and hopefully, Claire could help him. She just hoped they didn't send that annoying Frank Zambuco again.

"How do you know it's a homicide?" Norma interrupted Claire's train of thought.

Robby's brow ticked up. "What? You think he just fell into the pot and died on his own?"

Norma shrugged. "Stranger things have happened. Besides, who would want to kill someone in the middle of the Crab Festival?"

"That's a good question." Robby surveyed the crowd. "We'll need to find out just when the time of death was and then we'll need to know where all of you were at that time."

"Well, it couldn't have been any of us," Floyd Farner piped in from the back.

Robby squinted in his direction. "Why not?"

Floyd flapped his hands against his sides. "Any one of us would have to be out of our mind to kill someone and put them in the crab kettle. That's gonna put a real dampener on the festival and we all depend on the money."

"That's right," Lula Delgatto added. "The killer has to be an outsider."

"Not to mention that the crab kettle is a pretty dumb place to hide a body," Gus Weimar said. "Ain't none of us that dumb."

"Yeah, that's right," the crowd chorused.

"Sure. It wouldn't be an islander. We're smarter than that" Norma said quietly. "Unless whoever put it there wanted it to be found."

***

Dom noticed Claire shooting strange looks in his direction while they waited for the mainland police to show up. Or maybe his guilty conscience imagined it. He probably *should* have mentioned that he recognized the dead guy, but he didn't want to tie the man to Sarah.

But the way Claire was looking at him made him wonder if she had already made the connection. Then again, it could just be her zeal for investigating kicking in. Maybe she was sizing him up, trying to figure out his intentions. Perhaps she planned to help her nephew investigate the murder. It would be just like her to try to 'one-up' him and reveal the identity of the killer before he did.

Before he did? The thought made Dom realize that his subconscious had already been busy deciding that he was going to do his own investigation. He couldn't help it—investigating murder was in his blood. And the last investigation had made him feel so alive—it was the only thing that had made him feel that way since Sophia's death.

A large crowd had gathered by the time the police boat pulled up on the dock. Dom's stomach soured when he recognized the tall detective as the same one who had investigated the previous murder—Detective Frank Zambuco.

It wasn't that there was anything wrong with Zambuco. He was a good detective, in Dom's opinion, but he didn't like other people getting in on his investigation. Dom couldn't really fault him for that. After all, he'd been the same way when he was officially investigating. Still, it would be a lot more fun if they'd send someone more willing to listen to Dom's expert opinion, even if Dom was 'retired' now.

He watched Zambuco step off the boat, catching the toe of his size thirteen shoes on the edge of the dock and stumbling, then righting himself and spinning around toward the crowd. He whirled toward them, barking instructions to the three underlings he'd brought with him. Dom could almost feel the energy pouring off Zambuco, who seemed to possess an excess of it, especially for a guy who looked to be pushing sixty.

Zambuco looked at Robby. "What have we got?"

Robby nodded toward the kettle. "The festival committee found him when they did their inspection.

Zambuco walked to the edge of the grass and peered into the kettle. He snapped his sausage-like fingers in the direction of his underlings, who sprang into action taking out cameras and yellow folded plastic cards with numbers on them. He turned back to Robby. "Festival committee?"

Robby nodded in the direction of Dom, Claire, Tom, Norma, Jane and Mae.

Zambuco's narrowed eyes darted between Dom and Claire. "You two, again?"

Dom shrugged. "We like to keep active."

"Let's just make sure you don't keep active by butting in on my investigation." Zambuco gave them a warning glare then turned his attention back to Robby. "So who is the vic?"

"I wish I knew." Robby turned to the committee. "Do any of you recognize him?"

"No," they all said at once.

"Well, first thing we need to do is figure out how he died, and when. Then we gotta figure out who he is. Then maybe it will be clear who killed him." Zambuco snapped his head around to one of the docks where another boat was pulling up. "Oh, good. There's the medical examiner now. We can get this investigation rolling."

"Ahem." Someone cleared their throat and Zambuco cast an angry glare at the crowd. "Did someone want to say something?"

"Umm, well, we were just wondering if we can go on with the Crab Festival." Gus gestured toward all the tents. "We're all setup for it and everything."

Zambuco's eyes slid toward the tents. "You got hot dogs up there?"

"Yes."

Zambuco pivoted on his heels and looked at the crab kettle, then back at the tents.

"The crime scene is at the end of the pier here. I want to secure the last ten feet, but the rest of the tents can stay open as usual. You can have your festival, just don't let anyone past this point." He drew an imaginary line on the dock with his foot.

The medical examiner made her way up the doc and Zambuco greeted her, then handed her off to Robby. He looked over at Gus. "I guess I have time for a hot dog while Gladys does her job."

While Zambuco trotted off with Gus, Dom watched the police process the scene, paying particular attention to the clues they marked off and mentally gathering a few clues of his own. The medical examiner got right into the kettle to do her poking and prodding. By the time she was done, Zambuco had returned with a fresh mustard stain on his shirt.

Zambuco peered into the kettle and grimaced. "Did you find anything?"

"He's been dead about six hours. I'll have to get him back to the lab to know the exact time of death." Gladys signaled two other policemen who brought over a stretcher.

Dom glanced at his watch. Six hours put the time

of death around two a.m., a fact which he filed away for later use.

"Well, how did he die?" Norma demanded.

Gladys gestured to the kettle. "Lucky for him, he wasn't boiled."

"Was he battered?" someone from the crowd asked.

"No."

"Bludgeoned?"

"No."

"Bullet wound?"

"None of the above." Gladys stepped out of the kettle and let the two policemen in. They raised the body to hoist it out of the kettle and onto the stretcher.

"He was strangled." Gladys reached over and held up a piece of brown twine that dangled from the victim's neck.

Dom's heart skipped a beat. He tried to keep his face impassive so as not to let on that he recognized the twine as the same twine that Sarah had a ball of behind her counter back at *Chowders* … or at least he hoped she still had a ball of it back there.

He glanced over at Claire to see her mouth in a tight line. Her cheek twitched. He knew that look—Claire recognized the twine, too.

Chapter 5

Claire tried not gawk at the twine dangling from the medical examiner's hand. She arranged her face in a benign composure, as if she was looking at any other clue that had no significant meaning to her.

Except the twine did have significant meaning to her. It looked exactly like the twine Mae had showed them yesterday. The twine she used for her jam jars. The same jam jars that she'd dropped on the dock when she'd run into the tall, lanky—now deceased—guy.

Judging by the way Dom was looking at her, he recognized the twine, too. She snuck a look at Mae whose pale face stared in the direction of the medical examiner.

That proved to Claire that Mae didn't kill him—she looked stunned to see the man dead. Not that Claire needed proof. She already knew Mae couldn't have killed him. Claire was sure the look of shock was due to Mae's surprise at seeing the man dead and not to her surprise that there was still some evidence of the twine that had strangled him around his neck.

But why didn't Mae say she recognized him? Maybe she didn't know his name or anything about him. But Claire knew by the way they had been fighting that Mae must know something about the man. Maybe she was too shocked to speak up.

"Anyone recognize our deceased?" Zambuco blurted out.

A murmur ran through the crowd.

Claire looked at Mae.

Mae shut her mouth.

"I think I seen him down on the docks yesterday," Larry Gorham said.

Zambuco whirled on him. "Really? With who?"

Larry screwed up his mouth. "I'm not sure. He was down near the boat tours."

Zambuco squinted toward the longer docks on the far left where *Crabby* Tours and Barnacle Bob's parked their boats. The two businesses ran sightseeing and fishing boat trips for tourists and had a harsh rivalry going, each trying to win the bulk of the season's tourist business. It was a little awkward that they parked their boats near each other, but that was one of the longest docks and the shorter ones were reserved for individual fishing boats.

Claire wondered what the dead man had to do with them and if that had anything to do with his argument with Mae.

"That's a good enough place to start." Zambuco

watched them wheel the body away.

Indeed it was, Claire thought, surprising herself at how readily her mind took on the task of investigating the case. If she was honest, though, she was already coming up with a plan of action in her head because she was sure she wasn't the only one who had seen Mae argue with the man. She also knew that the twine around his neck would lead right to Mae as soon as anyone saw one of her newly designed jars of jam.

Zambuco wasn't from the island and he wouldn't protect Mae like she would, so she'd *have* to investigate.

She could practically hear Dom's brain humming beside her. She knew he would want to investigate, too. But Dom was a newcomer to the island and not loyal to Mae like she was, and there was no telling where his investigation would lead. She already knew he suspected something and he'd been in *Chowders* when Mae had shown them the twine.

And Dom was good. He could really throw a wrench into the works and that could be a problem if he suspected Mae. There was only one way to prevent that. As much as it pained her, she was going to have to team up with Dom to investigate the case. She just had to come up with some way to persuade him that it was his idea.

***

Their planned breakfast at *Chowders* had been ruined by the discovery of the body, so after Zambuco had done his round of questioning, Dom had gone home to his condo at the top of Israel Head Hill to indulge in one of his favorite breakfasts of Italian pastry.

He set a cannoli into the exact middle of a gold-rimmed, china dessert plate and cut it into five equal pieces, taking care not to crack the baked pastry shell. Setting his knife down one-quarter inch from the plate and at a perfect, ninety-degree angle to the edge of the table, he put one of the slices of cannoli on his fork and lifted it to his mouth, his tastebuds watering as he anticipated the contrast of the sweet center and crunchy outer shell.

As he chewed the creamy confection, he thought about the morning's events. He wondered who the mysterious man was.

Should he ask Sarah?

When he had asked before, she had brushed it off, claiming he was just a customer looking for pizza. But judging by the way they were arguing, Dom could tell that wasn't true. If he asked her again, though, it would seem like he was meddling in her personal business and he had the feeling Sarah was not going to confide in him.

And that was her right. It was, after all, none of his business, but the discovery of the body and the twine that had killed him didn't look good for Sarah. Dom didn't think she had killed the man, but it might be smart to find out where she was at the time of death and maybe even if she still had the ball of twine at *Chowders* so he could advise her on how to handle the police if they came sniffing around.

Dom had to admit, the prospect of entering into an investigation was exciting. But it was even more urgent that he clear Sarah because he had seen the way Claire was looking at that twine. He didn't know what else Claire knew about it, but he knew her well enough to know that she was going to start digging.

What if she discovered something that made Sarah look guilty? Would she tell her nephew?

Dom knew that Claire liked Sarah, but he also knew that she liked justice above all and if she thought Sarah had killed the strange man, she would have no qualms about stating her suspicions to the police, or even trying to prove them herself.

Dom took another bite of cannoli and chewed thoughtfully. His parakeets, Romeo and Juliet, tittered in the cage next to him.

"You don't think Sarah did it, do you?" he asked the birds.

Romeo tilted his head and looked down at Dom with intelligent black eyes. *"Tweetstigate."*

"Yes, I *am* going to investigate." Dom smiled. He must really be getting lonely. The bird's strange tweets were starting to sound like words.

He got up and looked in the drawer for a sprig of millet to clip to the side of the cage. Romeo, recognizing the drawer as the place where the millet treat was stored, paced back and forth on his perch, his green wings flapping. Juliet was more sedate. She never tweeted out words like Romeo did. In fact, she paid little attention to Dom. Right now, she was leaning against the side of the cage with her head tucked underneath her aqua and white wing, ignoring him.

Dom opened the cage door and clipped the millet spray onto the side. Romeo flew over, attacking the spray with his beak and sending seeds flying around the cage.

Juliet drew her head out from under her wing. Her shiny, black eyes darted from Dom to the millet spray.

"Go ahead. It's for you, too," he encouraged.

Juliet stretched her wings and sauntered over to the spray. Dom noticed that Romeo shuffled sideways to make room for her. What a gentleman.

Dom closed the door, leaving the two birds to eat their treat while he resumed eating his. Romeo flew to the side of the cage, his little pink claws grasping the bars as he hung upside down and looked at Dom quizzically.

"Cheeplaire."

"Yes, Claire could be a problem, couldn't she? But what can I do about it?"

"Tweenup."

Dom raised his brows at the bird. "That might not be a bad idea."

Claire was a good investigator, but Dom knew she could really throw a wrench into the works and that could be a problem if she suspected Sarah. There was only one way to prevent that. As much as it pained him, Dom was going to have to team up with Claire to investigate the case. He just had to come up with some way to persuade Claire that it was her idea.

Chapter 6

Claire looked over the railing at the edge of her garden for the twentieth time that day. Finally, Dom was sitting on the bench that overlooked Long Sands Beach where he usually sat when he wanted to contemplate things. She got in her Fiat and hurried down the hill.

She pulled in the parking lot casually, as if she had just happened to see him sitting on the bench while she was driving by. The truth was she'd been looking over her railing most of the afternoon, trying to catch him at just the right time to put her plan into action.

Dom turned at the sound of her approaching footsteps.

"Oh, hi, Claire. What brings you here?" He gestured for her to sit beside him on the bench and she did. He tipped the pink-striped bag he held in his hand toward her, offering her a pistachio which she declined. Pistachios were not part of her health regimen unless they were raw, which these were not.

"So, that was some find at the festival, huh?" Claire asked.

"Indeed, it was." Dom picked a pistachio out of the bag. "Do you have any idea who that guy was?"

Claire shook her head. "No idea at all."

"What about Robby? Have you talked to him? Does he know who it was?"

"You know how close-mouthed he can be. He hardly ever gives me any clues anymore."

"But we did get one clue at the crime scene," Dom said.

"That's right. The victim was seen down at the dock where the tour boats are."

"Yes. I wonder what he'd be doing there?"

Claire shrugged. "Who knows? Do you think his death had something to do with the boat tours?"

Dom's brows tugged together, forming a thick, gray line across his eyes. "I don't know. But I guess the way he was killed suggests some sort of an emotional element, doesn't it?" He glanced at Claire out of the corner of his eye.

Claire pressed her lips together. Investigating the emotional aspect of the cases was her forte, not Dom's. She would have to appeal to his sense of logical clues to get him excited about teaming up on the case. "I'm not so sure about that. I think the fact that he was put in the kettle is the real clue. I bet if the police follow that *logically*, they'll uncover the killer."

"So, you think it was someone from the island?"

Claire shook her head. "I doubt it. I mean, why would someone from the island put him in the kettle? What would their motive be? I noticed the police were putting down a lot of those yellow cards. I bet there was some interesting physical evidence there." Claire laughed. "But what am I telling you that for? You're the expert in that area. I bet you noticed every little detail yourself."

Dom straightened in the chair. A slight flush crept into his cheeks. He picked another pistachio out of the bag. "I might have noticed a few things. But someone must have been quite mad to strangle him. That's the part that's got me baffled. You know I'm not good at the human relationship aspect of investigations like you are."

Claire fidgeted in her seat, a swell of pride warming her chest. "I wonder what he was doing down there in the first place. He must have been killed early in the morning. We found him around eight and the ME said he had been dead about six hours."

Dom nodded slowly, then stared out to sea, timing his words so they would have the most impact on Claire. "I guess the police will question everyone as to their whereabouts and try to figure out a motive. You know Zambuco. He'll want to get the case closed as soon as possible. Do you think he'll try to nail someone from the island?"

Claire looked at him curiously. He sounded apprehensive, almost as if he took offense in Zambuco trying to pin it on an islander. Maybe he was becoming an islander himself ... and that would be a great way to get him to team up. "Probably. That's what he did last time

… but last time, we didn't let him get away with it. *We* found the real killer."

"That's right. We did good, but I'm afraid on this one, the emotional element would trip me up."

Claire frowned at him. "Oh, no, there's a much bigger problem with the physical clues .. This case needs your unique skills of logical deduction."

Dom nodded and they both let a few seconds pass before cautiously peering at each other out of the corner of their eyes.

"Our skills are complementary. That worked well on the last case. I suppose it could work on this one, too," Claire ventured, keeping her voice light as if it didn't make much of a difference to her whether they teamed up or not.

Dom twisted his lips and looked thoughtful, as if he hadn't considered the idea of them teaming up. "I suppose so. We did solve a lot of cases by putting our heads together down in Boston, and the last case on the island *was* kind of fun."

"It was," Claire said truthfully. She still hadn't forgotten the rush of capturing the killer and how it had made her feel useful and alive. "We do need to protect our own islanders from Zambuco and it seems we can best do that by working together."

"That's true." Dom cracked open a pistachio. "I suppose it can't hurt to team up. I was kind of looking for something to do anyway."

"It's settled, then. Where do we start?" Claire shifted in her seat to look at Dom. She'd purposely appealed to Dom's ego by asking him where he thought they should start. She already knew where *she* would start, but she didn't have a huge ego like he did and she figured that acting like she needed his input would insure his cooperation. She congratulated herself at how skillfully she'd maneuvered him into agreeing to work with her and even thinking it was his idea.

Dom chewed his pistachio. "Well, we need to find out the identity of the victim and what he was doing down at the pier early this morning."

"Didn't Larry say he had seen him down near the boat tours?" Claire's memory tingled. "I think I saw him talking to Donovan Hicks yesterday afternoon." She left out the part about him talking to Mae.

Dom looked at Claire sharply. "So you saw the victim yesterday? Did you mention it to Zambuco?"

Oops, she probably shouldn't have said that. "Well, yes. I mean, I think it was him. I was at the hairdresser and happened to be looking out at the dock. To tell you the truth, I didn't even really think about telling Zambuco. I mean, it's not like I know who he is or anything."

"But you did see him. What was he doing?"

Claire avoided eye contact. "Nothing. I just saw him talking to Donovan and then he walked off. They did seem like they were arguing, though."

Dom pressed his lips together and gazed out at the ocean. Donovan Hicks ran *Crabby* Cove Charters which had a fleet of tour boats and fishing boats. And fishing boats use twine. "Sounds like we need to go have a little talk with Donovan Hicks."

***

Donovan Hicks was on the *SeaStar*, one of *Crabby Tours*' sightseeing boats that took tourists on a round-trip excursion to the lighthouse at the end of the island and back. He was cleaning the boat out after its mid-afternoon trip. Claire and Dom weaved their way through the crowd of tourists disembarking from the boat, as they made their way down the dock toward it.

Donovan turned from his task of picking up the empty plastic cups left scattered on the wooden benches on the boat. "Hey, Claire." He nodded his chin at them. "Dom."

"Hi, Donovan. How you doing?" Claire stopped on the dock next to the boat and shaded her eyes from the sun to look up at him.

Beneath them, the water lapped at the thick pylons that held the dock in place. Dom watched a pair of ducks paddle leisurely under the dock, his eyes drifting to the other side, waiting for them to appear while he mentally congratulated himself on how skillfully he'd maneuvered Claire into agreeing to work with him. It seemed like she even thought it was her idea, which was perfect since that would make her more agreeable to work with.

Donovan came to the boat's railing, the brim of his captain's hat casting a shadow on his face as he looked down at them, his questioning eyes switching from Claire to Dom and back again. "Good. You guys fixin' to take a cruise?"

"Not today," Dom said, watching the ducks emerge on the other side. "We were wondering what you knew about the trouble this morning."

Donovan's eyes drifted to the grassy area at the end of the pier. "I heard 'bout that. Doesn't seem to have hurt the festival none, though."

Dom looked back at the long pier. It was crowded with tourists in colorful outfits, strolling along as if oblivious to the fact that someone had died there. Many of them probably were oblivious, since they'd likely only taken the ferry to the island for the day and weren't up on island news. But bad news traveled fast so many of them would have heard about it, as evidenced by the crowd around the yellow crime scene tape at the end of the picr.

"Did you know who he was?" Dom asked.

Donovan's eyes shot back to Dom's face. He hitched the left leg of his perfectly pressed navy blue Dockers up, put his foot on a bench and leaned his left elbow on his thigh. Dom wondered how he kept his clothes so clean—he always looked sharp and Dom expected tending to a cruise boat could get messy. He must have a big dry cleaning bill.

"Not really," Donovan said. "He was some developer guy come to the island to build some condos or something."

Claire's brows shot up. "Really? I didn't hear anything about any developer."

Donovan shrugged. "Not many people knew. I guess it was some sort of secret."

"So what was your business with him?" Dom asked.

"Business? I didn't have any business with him," Donovan answered.

"I thought I saw you arguing with him." Claire

watched Donovan like a hawk. Probably studying his body language, Dom thought. She was good at figuring out if people had something to hide just by looking at the way they stood and the gestures they made.

Dom thought it was all hooey, but he had to admit she *did* have a way of exposing people's motives and intentions through their behavior. But those little intuitions and feelings didn't hold up in court. Dom preferred hard evidence. His gaze slid to the boat docked next to the *SeaStar*, the *Crabby Ellen*. It was a fishing boat and in the back of it, he could see a fishing net made out of twine that was very similar to that found on the victim.

Donovan said, "We didn't argue. I think you must be mistaken."

Dom looked back at Donovan, who was now frowning at Claire.

Claire narrowed her eyes. "I thought it looked like you had words."

Donovan chuckled. "Oh, well, you might have thought that. We were talking about baseball and it got a little heated. Can you believe he's a Yankees fan?"

Claire snorted. Everyone knew Donovan was a rabid Red Sox fan. He'd gotten into many arguments defending them, but as far as Dom knew, none of those had ended in murder.

Dom pointed to the back of the *Crabby Ellen*. "Do you use that fishing twine on all your fishing boats?"

Donovan glanced over. "Yeah. We always use the biodegradable."

"Different colors?" Dom asked.

"What? Oh, no we always use the blue. It matches with our boats." Donovan leaned over and tapped the side of the freshly painted *SeaStar* to illustrate. It was, indeed, blue. Dom remembered how proud Donovan had been at the beginning of the season when he'd gotten new paint jobs for the fleet of boats, and shirts for the crew to match.

Dom glanced at Claire to see if she picked up on why he was asking. He hated to call attention to the importance of the twine, but Claire wasn't stupid and she'd seen the twine around the victim's neck. She didn't seem overly interested in his line of questioning, though, so he continued. "You don't use the brown on any of your boats?"

Donovan's eyes flicked across the dock to Barnacle Bob's fleet of boats. Dom followed his gaze. Barnacle Bob had fishing boats, too, and Dom would wager they had twine nets in them.

"Nope. I always use the blue." Donovan removed his foot from the bench and bent over to pick up another plastic cup.

Dom noticed one of the kids from the island, Bradley Sears, washing down Barnacle Bob's fishing boat, the *Last Catch*, on the other side of the dock. Bradley was one of the island kids who Dom sometimes entertained with stories of his past cases.

"Okay, well, nice talking to you," Dom said to Donovan, who had already gone back to his clean-up task.

Dom looked at Claire and jerked his head toward the *Last Catch*. She nodded and they walked across the wide dock.

"Hey, Bradley," Dom called out to the teen.

Bradley turned, his face cracking into a smile when he saw Dom. He turned off the hose and came over to the railing of the boat.

"Hey, Mr. Benedetti. That's something about the murder, huh?" Bradley's voice raised an octave with excitement. Or maybe it was puberty. Either way, Dom could tell Bradley thought the murder was interesting. "This place is getting to be a real homicide magnet. I think you guys will catch the killer, right?"

Bradley's innocent, wide eyes ping-ponged back and forth between Claire and Dom, who exchanged an uneasy glance. Apparently, the last case had given them a reputation for solving the island's crimes and Dom wasn't sure if that would help them or hinder them with this one. He wasn't sure if he wanted the whole island knowing they were investigating it. He certainly didn't want it to get back to Zambuco, who seemed to take a dim view of civilians butting in.

"Maybe," Dom said. "We were wondering if Bob is around."

Bradley's brows shot up. "You think he's mixed up in this?"

Dom laughed. "No, of course not. We just heard the victim was down on the dock here and wanted to know if Bob had seen him."

Bradley's face fell. "Oh. Well, Mr. Cleary hasn't shown up for work yet today."

That piqued Dom's interest. "Really? Is that unusual?"

"Yeah. He's usually here bright and early."

Claire had moved down the dock and was looking in the back of the boat. She tilted her head slightly and Dom walked over. A fishing net lay in the back of the boat … and it was made out of brown twine.

Chapter 7

Claire had mixed feelings about the discovery of the twine in the back of Barnacle Bob's boat, not to mention the fact that he hadn't shown up for work as usual that morning. She certainly didn't want Bob to be the killer, but at least now they had an angle to follow that didn't lead to Mae Biddeford.

Claire had promised to go to the festival with Jane, so she dropped Dom off at his car at the lookout bench, then picked up Jane and parked behind the beauty shop.

Apparently, the recent murder hadn't put a dampener on the Crab Festival because the pier was swarming with tourists. Claire and Jane strolled past the tents, inhaling the tangy smell of fried clams and listening to the clamor of the crowd.

"Have you heard anything from Robby about the …" Jane tilted her head in the direction of yellow crime scene tape at the end of the pier. "Incident."

Claire glanced down through the throng of tourists. Although the rest of the festival was going on as usual, there would be no crab boil today. The police had finished processing the scene and cordoned off the area with an overabundance of yellow crime scene tape. Instead of scaring tourists away, it had acted as a magnet, attracting them to the end of the pier where they could gawk and point.

Claire watched a throng of seagulls flap noisily above the giant pot which had been too heavy for the police to take. There were no crabs in the pot, but the gulls still squawked loudly, probably angry that they were getting robbed of the scraps of the boil that tourists usually threw to them. There would be no more crab boils until they got a new pot.

"I haven't heard a thing." Claire shifted her gaze to the dock where *Crabby* Tours and Barnacle Bob's had their boats. "We did go down and talk to Donovan Hicks earlier this morning because Larry said the victim had been seen down there."

"Did you find anything out?"

Claire shrugged. "Not really, though we do need to follow up with Bob. He wasn't in when we were there."

Claire knew from experience that it wasn't a good idea to let out too much information from the investigation—even to her best friend. People tended to jump to conclusions and that was never helpful, so she didn't mention the twine or the fact that Bob had been unusually late.

They continued down the pier, passing the various

vendors, most of whom they'd known all their lives. Claire paused in front of Sally Kimmel's florist tent. Colorful, lush flowers filled the tent and the scent of lilacs wafted out. It looked gorgeous, as usual.

Sally was a gifted floral designer and Donovan's sister. Claire wondered if she should go in and ask some questions, but she really didn't know exactly what to ask. Sally was one of the few family members who didn't work in the *Crabby* Tours business so she probably wouldn't have had any idea why Donovan had been talking to the victim.

Jane had paused in front of the *Harbor Fudge Shop* tent across from Sally's. She looked at Claire with a mischievous gleam in her eye. "Well, *I* found something out."

"You did? What?"

"The victim's name."

"Do tell." Claire was tired of thinking of him as 'the victim'. A name would be most welcome.

"Milton Blunt."

Claire pressed her lips together. "Never heard of him."

"Me, either." Jane pulled Claire into the *Fudge Shop* tent. "Come on, I know you love the dark chocolate bark."

"Did you find out anything else about him?" Claire went straight to a glass display case that had slabs of chocolate so dark they were almost black. Claire had quite the sweet tooth, but dark chocolate was the only dessert that she allowed herself to indulge in because it offered a variety of health benefits. She pointed to a batch of bark studded with almonds and held up two fingers.

"Not a thing. Just that he was a real estate developer." Jane squatted down in front of a display of soft-centered chocolates and tilted her head to read the descriptions on the sides of the boxes.

Jane picked out a box and then beat Claire to the cash register, insisting on paying for both their purchases. Claire graciously accepted, although she didn't like it when Jane paid. She knew Jane didn't make much on her post office salary and Claire had plenty of money. But Jane had her pride and Claire didn't want to wound it, even though she knew Jane needed the money now more than ever.

Claire broke off a small piece of the bark and put it in her mouth, savoring the bittersweet taste of the chocolate as it melted on her tongue. "How's your mom?"

Jane's face pinched and Claire kicked herself for bringing it up. Jane's ninety-three-year-old mother had been diagnosed with Alzheimer's a year earlier and it had killed Jane not to be able to keep her at home and care for her herself. Luckily, she had been able to get her into a very exclusive—and expensive —assisted-living facility. Claire wondered where Jane found the money for that, but had the good sense not to be rude enough to ask.

"She's doing okay." Jane's eyes glistened, making Claire feel even worse. "She gets incredible care where she is, so I'm lucky to be able to keep her there."

"You did the right thing," Claire soothed.

"I know." Jane looked away and Claire searched for

more words to lift her sweet friend's spirits. Jane was the kind of person who always had something nice to say, the kind of friend that lifted you up and always looked on the bright side. Claire wished she could be as positive and sweet as her friend, but she was more suspicious in nature.

A yellow blur rushing into the tent caught her eye. "What the—"

Jane's reaction was quicker than Claire's and she jumped to the side, blocking the passage of the exuberant golden retriever puppy.

"Whoa, there." Jane picked the puppy up, smiling as it licked her face. "Where did you come from?"

"Probably the animal rescue tent." Mooseamuck Island was home to many animal lovers, Claire included. They had a very good animal rescue operation and a tent was set up at every festival to show off the animals looking for homes.

"Let's bring him back." Jane struggled to hold the wiggly puppy in her arms as they headed down the pier. Claire's spirits lifted for her friend—nothing like a puppy to take your mind off your troubles.

The animal rescue was five tents down—a big, red sign stood out in front. Claire saw a swoosh of blonde hair disappear around the back of the tent and then she was distracted by Mae Biddeford darting out of the opening with a harried expression on her face. Mae glanced left, then right, then noticed Claire and Jane coming toward her with the puppy.

"Oh, there he is." Mae's face lightened with relief. "I'm so sorry. He just ran out. I don't know where Sarah's gone off to. She's supposed to be helping me."

Sarah appeared from the side of the tent. "Sorry, I'll take him." She held her arms out to take the puppy from Jane, her face breaking into a wide smile as the puppy settled into her arms and licked her face exuberantly.

Claire's heart warmed at the rare expression of pure joy on Sarah's face. Claire knew something weighed heavily on the young woman and, as a result, she rarely smiled. A puppy seemed like just the thing Sarah needed.

"Are you going to adopt him?" Claire asked.

Regret washed over Sarah's fine features as she put the puppy down in a playpen filled with three others just like him. "No, I can't. I mean, I have the restaurant and all."

"You need to take more days off from that restaurant. Then you might have more time and won't have to sneak off to meet young men at the festivals," Mae teased with a mischievous smile on her face.

Sarah's face tightened. "I wasn't … I mean … I'm sorry, it won't happen again."

Claire felt sorry for Sarah, but she really didn't need to act so upset when Mae was obviously teasing. Claire figured she must have been meeting Shane McDonough behind the tent. She'd seen the way the two of them looked at each other, but why meet in secret? She didn't see any reason for it. They were often seen together at the restaurant and it was no secret that they were very close.

"Meow!"

Claire looked down to see the Maine Coon cat that

frequently appeared at her patio door. "Is this cat up for adoption?"

"Oh, no. That's Porch Cat. You know him, don't you?" Mae asked. "He's just making the rounds."

Mae held out a small, orange, square cat treat and Porch Cat sniffed it thoroughly before deciding it was okay to eat. He gently took it from Mae and ate it, making little crunching sounds.

Porch Cat looked up at Claire and winked, then turned and trotted out of the tent, flicking his tail in the direction of a tent across on the opposite side of the pier and two spaces down. Claire looked in that direction and saw it was Barnacle Bob's tent and he was in it.

Claire grabbed Jane's arm. "Let's go over there. I have a question for Bob."

Jane gave the golden retriever puppy one last scratch behind the ears, and they said good-bye to Mae and Sarah, then headed to the other tent.

Inside, several large displays highlighted the different boats in Barnacle Bob's fleet and the tours they offered. In the middle was a podium where Bob's daughter, Lisa, was taking cruise reservations.

Bob peered over Lisa's shoulder at the reservation book. He was in his late fifties, tall with skin that was leathery from years on the ocean running the family business. He usually looked fit and healthy, but today his unshaven face was pale and haggard with dark circles under his eyes.

"Hey, Bob. Rough night?" Claire asked.

Bob's head jerked up and he fixed red-rimmed eyes

on Claire. "I'll say. I haven't felt this under the weather in a long time."

"Do you have that flu that's going around?" Claire asked.

Bob ducked his head. "I wish I could say that was it, but I have to admit I had a bit too much to drink last night and I slept in. Haven't done that since I was in my twenties."

Claire laughed. "I remember sleeping in a few times when I was that young, too. But it's not like you to tie one on."

Bob glanced at Lisa. "Certainly not. I actually didn't even think I drank that much, but judging by the way I feel this morning, I must have."

"Where were you drinking?"

Bob scrunched his face up as if trying to remember where he had been drinking was painful. "I remember starting out at *Duffy's Tavern*. I only went in for a beer to celebrate my divorce." He looked sheepishly at Lisa. "Anyway, someone kept putting drinks in front of me and I kept drinking them. After that, the next thing I remember is waking up. I guess I'm a lightweight when it comes to drinking. I'm usually only good for a couple of beers."

Claire felt a pang of sympathy. Bob was acting like the divorce was no biggie, but she knew how crushed he was when Molly hit him with those divorce papers last year.

"I'm sorry about the divorce," she said.

Bob shrugged. "Ah, it's nothing now. We been separated a long time and we've both moved on."

"So, you must have closed *Duffy's*, then," Claire prompted.

Bob rubbed his hands down his face. "I guess so. The truth is, I don't remember. I know I was there and then I was in my bed. My car was still in the fishermen's lot over there." Bob nodded toward a small lot which was reserved for the cars of the fishermen who owned boats at the dock. "So I guess I musta' walked home. Either way, I won't be doing that again."

"Getting divorced or tying one on?" Lisa quipped dryly.

"Neither." Bob glanced at his watch. "I gotta run. Got ten minutes before the next cruise and I gotta captain it."

Claire watched him sprint down the dock, her heart twisting. She liked Bob. He was a good guy, a family man who had worked hard at his business. But he'd just admitted he was drunk and couldn't remember where he was last night *and* he had the same brown twine in his boat that had killed Melvin Blunt.

In Claire's book, that made him a key suspect ... the only question was *why* would Bob Cleary want to kill a real estate developer?

Chapter 8

The next morning, Dom sat at the Formica table in *Chowders*, mulling over what Claire had told him about her conversation with Bob Cleary at the Crab Festival.

Bob had all the makings of a primary suspect, but they needed more information. What was his motive? What exactly were his movements that night? They'd agreed not to ask Robby anything about the case just yet, so they'd need to rely on town gossip to get their answers … and breakfast time with the locals at *Chowders* was the perfect time to do that.

Dom tapped his finger on the side of his warm coffee mug, letting the sounds of sizzling bacon and clattering dishes fade to the background as he thought about the case and waited for the others to show up.

He'd tried to finagle a way to find out if the ball of twine was still behind the counter, but Sarah had been preoccupied. Not her usual talkative self. She'd practically ignored him and he didn't want to seem pushy. It was a minor point, anyway—surely most anyone could buy twine like that. He made a mental note to check that out.

Dom poured some more cream into his coffee mug and watched it swirl around while he fought off the doubts that crowded his mind. He now knew the victim's name was Milton Blunt, but he hadn't done any research on him so he had no idea who he was or why he was on Mooseamuck Island. Would he be able to figure out why he was killed or who the killer was without the same type of access to information that he'd had when he'd been a consultant to the police? He was much older now—his skills, perhaps, not as sharp. What if he couldn't figure it out?

But he *had* figured out who the killer was in the murder they'd had earlier that spring. Grudgingly, he had to admit it had been with Claire's help. And he'd probably need her help now, too. The thought of it prickled his nerves. But he had to admit it hadn't been quite as annoying to work with her on the last case they'd solved here on the island as it had been back in Boston all those years ago. Maybe old age had tempered him.

"Penny for your thoughts."

The voice made him jump. He looked up to see Claire slip onto the chair across from him. She raised a brow, a slight smile curling her lips. "I guess you were deep in thought."

Dom lowered his voice to a whisper. "I was thinking about what you said about Bob. We need more information."

"I know. We'll have to ask around." Claire glanced around the restaurant. It was quickly filling up with locals and Dom assumed she didn't want them all to overhear and figure out they were investigating. Smart.

He spotted Norma, Jane, and Mae coming in the door and inclined his head slightly. Claire looked at the door, saw them too, pressed her lips together and nodded. They'd have to talk shop about the case some other time.

"You two talking about the murder?" Norma asked in her usual, blunt manner as the three of them sat at the table.

"We were talking about the weather," Claire said. "Why? Did you hear something?"

"Something about what?" Tom Landry appeared at Claire's elbow, taking the seat beside her. Claire noticed it just happened to be the seat across from Mae.

"The murder." Norma waved impatiently at the waitress who headed toward them, pulling a notepad from her pocket.

They ordered—egg whites and whole wheat toast for Dom, oatmeal for Claire and a variety, ranging from pancakes to fruit salad, for the others.

While they waited for their breakfast, they talked about the Crab Festival. Claire pulled the basket of teabags from the center of the table and started rooting through it. Alice pulled her knitting needles out of her bag. She was knitting something with thick, heavy yarn. Dom glanced out the window at the bright pink sun over the ocean and started to itch just thinking about wearing whatever wooly garment Alice was knitting, especially when the day promised to be a scorcher. Eventually, the conversation turned to the murder.

"Well, I'm sure there are people right here in the restaurant who are glad that man is dead," Alice said matter-of-factly.

Dom snapped his head in her direction, then glanced nervously at the kitchen where Sarah was busy chopping. Did Alice know something about Sarah's fight with Milton Blunt?

Claire looked up from her job of dunking the tea bag into her mug, her brow creased into a 'v'. "What do you mean, Alice?"

"Well, you know who he was, don't you?" Alice kept her eyes on her knitting, her needles clacking in perfect rhythm as she talked.

"No."

Alice wound a strand of purple yarn over one needle, pulled the other through and then looked up from her work. "Mae, Tom ... I know you do."

Claire's head jerked around to look at Mae and Tom. Dom's eyebrows tingled with interest at this new development.

Norma smacked her hand on the table. "Who the *heck* was he?"

Mae and Tom stared at each other like deer caught in the headlights.

"You guys don't know?" Real estate agent Josie Learner leaned over from the next table. Apparently, she'd been listening to their conversation and was eager to fill them in.

"No," Dom and Claire both said.

"That was Milton Blunt." She paused and Claire and Dom both nodded. They already knew his name. "He's a big real estate developer. He's had his eye on some land here to develop into condos for years. The owners have refused his offers, but this time he'd decided to stay on the island for good. He said he wasn't going to take no for an answer."

"What property is that?" Dom ventured.

"The farms of Mae Biddeford and Tom Landry."

***

Claire dropped her teabag, the string disappearing into the steaming cup of tea. She stared at Mae. Why hadn't Mae mentioned that before? Her gaze slid over to Tom. Or Tom for that matter. If Blunt had been making them offers on their properties, surely they would have recognized him yesterday morning?

Across the table, Mae fidgeted in her seat. Tom's eyes were glued to his pancakes as if making sure the little pieces soaked up just the right amount of maple syrup was the most important task in the world.

"Neither of you recognized the victim yesterday?" Dom's eyes drifted from Mae to Tom.

"Well, I barely got a look at him," Mae said. "It was ghastly. When the coroner moved him, I just barely saw a contorted face and I had to turn away."

Claire remembered how Mae had shown up late for the meeting that morning. Why *was* she late?

Tom shrugged. "I thought it might be him," he stuttered. "But I couldn't be sure and I didn't want to say."

"Well, ain't that a hoot." Norma slapped the table. "Sounds like you guys have a good motive."

Claire shot Norma an angry look. Did she have to go and say *that*? She could see the comment had garnered Dom's interest, but she was sure he would have picked up on the motive anyway, so she couldn't really blame Norma too much.

Dom cast a frowning glance over at the door and Claire spun around. Zambuco.

The room fell silent as the tall detective waltzed in. Claire was glad to see he'd changed his mustard-stained shirt. This time he was wearing a pink knit shirt with tan chinos. The man had no fashion sense.

His eyes drifted around the room, then came to rest on Claire's table. He lurched in their direction, whistling what sounded like marching band music under his breath.

"I figured I'd find you all here." Zambuco tapped on the edge of the table with his thick fingers. The waitress came over and raised an eyebrow at him. "I'll have a root beer. Lots of ice."

"What can we do for you, Detective?" Claire asked innocently.

Zambuco zeroed in on her with his beady, dark eyes. "Have you been going around asking questions about the murder?"

"Of course not," Claire said. "We're just sitting here eating breakfast. The murder is the furthest thing from our minds."

Zambuco scowled at the entire table, making everyone fidget. Claire could feel the other diner patrons staring at them.

"Would you like to join us?" Jane, always polite, scooted her chair over and indicated for Zambuco to pull a chair from the other table and sit next to her.

Zambuco's face softened as he looked at Jane. Claire frowned at the flush on Jane's cheeks. Claire's eyes flew back to Zambuco. He was still looking at Jane.

Claire wasn't sure, but the looks on both of their faces seemed to indicate they were regarding each other as much more than detective and potential witness. Claire pushed the thought out of her mind. She was sure her dear, sweet, graceful friend would not be interested in the annoying, overbearing, klutzy Zambuco. Jane was just being polite.

Zambuco tore his gaze from Jane and fixed it on Mae, his face now all hard lines and his eyes sharp. "I hear you had an adversarial relationship with the victim."

"I … well, I wouldn't say that it was adversarial. *Or that it was even a relationship*," Mae said indignantly.

"But he wanted to buy your family farm, isn't that correct?"

Mae pursed her lips and nodded primly. "That is correct. But my farm is not for sale."

The root beer came and Zambuco grabbed it from the waitress. The ice cubes clinked together as he chugged half of it down. "I hear he was putting the pressure on."

Mae patted her lips with her napkin and then threw it over her half-finished breakfast. "I don't know what you mean."

Zambuco turned his attention on Tom Landry. "And I heard the same of you."

Tom looked up from his pancakes. "He offered and I refused."

"And did he accept your refusals and go away, or did he try more persuasive techniques?" Zambuco asked. "I heard Blunt liked to play hardball."

Crash!

The dishes smashing in the kitchen tore Zambuco's attention away from Mae's face and Claire was grateful for that because if he'd seen the way her face crumbled, he might have pulled her into the station for questioning right then and there.

Claire glanced at the kitchen to see a red-faced Sarah staring down at her feet. Sarah looked out at the dining room and shrugged. "Sorry, they slipped."

Claire's heart warmed as she watched Shane McDonough slide his arm around Sarah's shaking shoulders.

"I'll pick them up," he said. "You get back to cooking."

Claire couldn't help the smile that tugged at the corners of her lips. Shane was a fourth generation islander, a real looker and an all-around good guy. He was a carpenter, but she'd noticed he'd been spending more time in Sarah's kitchen helping her than out building additions over the past year. She could see the two had a budding romance and was happy for Sarah.

Claire thought Sarah was way too serious for her young age. She knew Sarah's demeanor had a lot to do with the deep, dark secret she harbored and she was glad

Sarah had Shane to help ease that burden—even if she hadn't shared that secret with Shane, Claire knew from her years as a psychologist that having someone who genuinely cared for you helped even if you couldn't tell them all your problems.

Dom hadn't been distracted by the crash like Zambuco. Sure, he was looking in the direction of the crash, too, but Claire could tell by the way he was patting his eyebrows that he was already adding Mae, and probably Tom, to *his* suspect list.

Zambuco brought his attention back to the table. Thankfully, Mae had recovered.

"Well, he wasn't a nice man, if that's what you mean," she said.

Tom nodded his head in agreement. "No. Not nice at all."

Claire noticed Tom and Mae exchange a look. They were probably just as surprised as she was that they had agreed on something. The two of them were always arguing about something, with Mae claiming Tom's goats ate her berries and Tom claiming Mae planted on his land. She hadn't known them to agree on anything since first grade, but apparently a common enemy gave them a bond.

"And did you have an altercation with Mr. Blunt?" Zambuco persisted.

Mae shook her head.

Claire remembered the argument she'd seen the day before on the dock. Why was Mae keeping it a secret? Then again, considering the man just turned up dead, it probably was smarter to keep it secret.

Guilt gnawed at Claire's chest. Part of her deep down inside was still a police consultant and that part knew she should speak up about the argument she had witnessed. It was the right thing to do.

But another part of her remembered the murder case earlier that spring when she'd seen Norma fighting with the victim. She'd been forced to tell Zambuco that she'd witnessed the fight, thus casting Norma onto his suspect list. That hadn't gone well for Norma, and Claire had been guilt-ridden over it. She pressed her lips together and looked down at her oatmeal. She wasn't going to make the same mistake of betraying a friend again.

Claire noticed the look of concentration on Dom's face. He was probably picturing Mae as the killer. But Mae couldn't have done it. She was too small and she was an old lady. There was no way she could have wrestled Blunt into that crab pot. Tom, on the other hand, was still strong and wiry. He labored on the farm every day and had muscles of a man thirty years his junior. He could have done it. But Claire didn't want to think about that. Tom was one of the sweetest, most gentle men she knew. He was no killer.

Norma thumped her cane on the floor to get Zambuco's attention. "So you mean this Blunt guy just came to town to try to steal the farms from these poor folks?" Norma fixed her sharp glare on Zambuco. "No wonder someone killed him. Sounds like he deserved it."

Claire was surprised to see the corners of Zambuco's lips twitch upward. Was he actually going to smile?

"Ahhh, Ms. Hopper. Did you know the deceased? I seem to recall you were a suspect in our last murder."

Norma laughed. "You'd like for it to be me, wouldn't you? That would make it easy. But I must confess, I didn't know him."

Something didn't sit right with Claire. If Blunt was here for Mae and Tom's land, why was he spending so much time down at the docks? She was desperate to get the spotlight off of Mae and Tom.

"I heard quite a few people say they saw him down on the docks. What business would he have down there if he was here to try to persuade Mae and Tom to sell their land?" Claire asked. "And what was he doing down there in the wee hours of the morning the day he was killed?"

Zambuco rasied his voice and turned to face the whole diner to include them in his invitation. "I was hoping one of *you* could tell *me* that."

"I know why," Josie chimed in from the next table. Heads swiveled in her direction.

"Why?" Zambuco jiggled the cubes in his empty glass—an apparent signal to the waitress to get a refill.

Josie straightened her spine and primped her hair, obviously enjoying the attention. "He *was* looking to build condos on the Biddeford and Landry farms, but he also had another business venture that he was going to start right away. In fact, he'd just signed a longterm rental lease for the property."

"What property is that?"

"The long dock at the end of the pier. He was going to open a tour boat charter. He said it was going to be so spectacular that it would put the other tour boat charters out of business."

Chapter 9

Dom leaned his hip against his car in the *Chowders* parking lot. The sun had heated the metal and he could feel it burning through his pants. He shifted his weight away from the car as he watched a myriad of emotions travel across Claire's face.

"You can't mean that you think Mae or Tom did it?" she was saying.

Dom shook his head. He was well aware that the islanders stuck up for each other and he knew Claire would not accept them easily as suspects. The truth was, he didn't really think they did it, either. He couldn't tell if that was his investigator's gut instinct or if he was becoming an 'islander' himself and adopting their protective nature for one another.

He cautioned himself to ignore any emotions or attachments he had to the suspects and go only on the physical evidence and clues. It was doubtful the senior citizens killed Blunt, but he'd seen people do much worse before, when their family heritage was threatened.

"I'm not saying I think they did it. I'm just saying they both have a motive. It's just something we need to look into in order to make sure we do a thorough *and impartial* investigation," he said.

"Right. Exactly." Claire seemed mollified by his words. "I just wish we knew what the police knew."

Dom whistled through his teeth. "No kidding. Maybe it's time to pay Robby a visit. Do you think he would share anything with us?"

"I don't know. He does kind of owe us after the last murder when we gave him credit for capturing the killer. But Zambuco will be mad if he finds out Robby shared evidence with us and I don't want to jeopardize his job. Then again, an aunt does have a right to visit her favorite nephew any time she wants, doesn't she?"

Dom laughed. "Of course. No one could blame her for that."

They were silent for a few minutes, each turning over the news of Blunt's real reason to be on the island in their minds. Dom listened to the sound of gravel crunching under tires as the last of the breakfast-goers pulled out of the lot. A movement by the window caught his eye. He looked up to see Sarah frowning out at them. She caught him looking and ducked back in.

Claire had noticed it, too. "Sarah seems awfully out of sorts. Is something wrong with her?"

Dom shrugged. "Maybe she's mad because I told her the tiramisu needed more mascarpone."

Dom had noticed Sarah seemed out of sorts, too, but he didn't think it had anything to do with the mascarpone. He'd thought it had to do with the fight she'd had with Blunt. But apparently Sarah didn't have ties to him or Zambuco would have mentioned it in the diner. Dom had to admit he was relieved that there were other suspects who were more interesting than Sarah. After all, all Sarah had done was argue with the guy—Mae, Tom, Donovan and Bob had much more compelling reasons to want Blunt dead.

But if Sarah didn't know Blunt, why the argument? Maybe Blunt really did just go in there for pizza. It sounded like he was a jerk, so having a temper tantrum over not being able to get pizza might not be so farfetched. And if that were the case, there was no reason to tell Claire about the argument he'd witnessed. When he was consulting for the police, he would never have kept something like that from his partner, even if the detail clearly had nothing to do with the case, like this one. He wasn't consulting and Claire wasn't his partner, but still, the pang of guilt gnawed at his stomach, threatening to spoil his breakfast.

"I also think we should research the victim," Claire was saying. "He doesn't sound like he was very nice. He may have made a lot of enemies and any one of them could've come to the island to do him in."

"That's a good idea. And I think we need to go back to the dock and talk to Donovan and Bob. Their businesses were threatened by his new business venture."

"And Bob Cleary doesn't have a very good alibi for that night. He was drunk in the bar by his own admission. He doesn't even remember how we got home."

Dom looked up at the clear, blue sky. The smell of home fries from breakfast still lingered in the air, even though it was mid-morning. "The charter boats will probably be out right now. I don't think we'll be able to catch Donovan or Bob, but maybe we can do something even better."

"What's that?"

"Find out what really happened in *Duffy's Tavern* that night."

***

Duffy's Tavern had been a local watering hole for as long as Claire could remember. It sat on a side street, parallel to the pier, in an old, brick building with a large, iron-hinged oak door.

Claire was going to burst if she drank another cup of tea, but she ordered one anyway. It was too early for beer. She slid her small, square napkin around on the polished oak bar as she waited for the bartender, Emile, to pour the hot water into a mug. Her nose wrinkled slightly at the faint smell of bleach that wafted up from the smooth surface of the bar.

One small window in the front, home to a lone, wilting plant, let a shaft of light in which illuminated the liquor bottles lined up behind the bar in jewel tones of red, amber and blue. On a typical Saturday night, one would have to shout to be heard above the din, but at mid-morning on a Sunday, the tavern was pretty much empty. The only sounds came from old-timer Floyd

Green who sat at the end of the bar with a newspaper spread out in front of him, cracking peanut shells and flipping the peanuts into his mouth in a rhythmic cadence. A tumbler filled with dark liquid, which Claire hoped was just cola, rested by his right hand.

"We were wondering if you saw Bob Cleary here Friday night," Dom asked after Emile slid steaming mugs across the bar to both of them.

"Yeah. I remember Bob being here Friday night." Emile worked a white bar cloth around the rim of a glass. He held the glass up to the light, squinted at it, then put it down and grabbed another. "I've never quite seen him like that before."

"You mean drunk?" Claire asked.

Emile nodded. "Usually just comes in for a few beers."

"How many drinks did he have?" Dom asked.

Emile stopped polishing and looked out at the room. "You know, I didn't think he had that many, but I really wasn't watching. It was busy in here with everyone winding down after a hard day of setting up the tents for the Crab Festival."

"Bob said someone kept sending drinks over to him. Any idea who that was?" Claire asked.

Emile shook his head. "Like I said, I was too busy to pay attention."

Dom took a cautious sip from his mug. "Do you know who Bob talked to that night?"

"Sure. He talked to lots of people—Donovan Hicks, Tom Landry, Gus Stevens, Larry Gorham."

"How long did he stay?"

"A little past midnight, I think."

"How'd he get home? Did he leave with someone?"

Emile twisted his face in thought. "I think Shane drove him. He was one of the few sober people in the bar."

"Shane?" Dom's bushy eyebrows dipped inwards. "You mean Shane McDonough, Sarah White's boyfriend?"

"Yep."

Claire slid a sideways glance at Dom. Did Dom think Shane was mixed up in this? "Was Bob angry? Did he get in a fight with anyone?"

Emile made a face. "Bob? No. You know how he is. Not much gets him riled up."

"Maybe you were too busy to notice," Dom suggested.

"It wasn't Bob that got into it Friday night," Floyd cut in.

Claire swiveled her head toward Floyd. "What do you mean? Did someone else get into a fight? Who?"

Floyd picked a peanut out of the shell, tilted his head back, tossed it into his mouth, then deposited the empty shell in a bowl. He rubbed his hands together and turned his attention back to Claire. "Yep. The ball game was on and everyone was getting a little worked up about it. We were having a good old time cussing out Jeter and the Yankees. Some outsider was sittin' on the stool next to me and he got real worked up. I guess he doesn't like them. Anyway, things were getting a little rowdy when that blond guy came in and really boiled the outsider over."

"Outsider? Do you know who it was?" Claire asked.

"Some tall, lanky guy. Acted like he owned half the island, but I never saw him before." Floyd started patting down the pockets in his fishing vest. "He gave me a card and I might have kept it. Or I might have tossed it. Tell the truth, he was a pompous bore so I had no reason to keep it."

Claire slid a sideways glance at Dom. The description sounded like Blunt.

"Who was the blond guy?" Dom asked.

Floyd finished with his vest pockets, stood and started looking through his pants pockets. "Some guy staying over at the *Gull View Inn*. Darn tourists. Ruining the island, if you ask me. Don't even know how to act civil in a bar."

"So, what did they fight about?" Claire asked.

"I couldn't hear all of it, but the blond guy, he was hot under the collar. He came over to the other guy and tapped him on the shoulder right after the game-winning home run." Floyd pulled out his wallet and started removing things, placing each item one by one on the bar. Ticket stubs, pictures, a dollar bill, fishing line.

"Did they actually get into a fist fight?" Dom slid his eyes over to Emile, who shook his head.

"There wasn't any fist fight, but I remember keeping my eye on the two of them just in case," Emile said. "The young guy's body language suggested he might throw a punch, but he didn't. It was a short exchange."

"That's right" Floyd said, his eyes on his wallet which he was still emptying onto the bar. "The older guy was acting all cocky and self-satisfied, almost as if he was challenging the younger guy. I remember the young guy said something about finishing off the job 'she' started and the older guy just started laughing. It wasn't no pleasant-sounding laugh, either."

"Then what happened?" Claire asked.

"The blond guy got all red in the face. I thought he was gonna haul off and hit the other guy, but he turned around and stomped out." Floyd squinted at a thin card he'd taken out of his wallet. "Yep, here it is right here. This here's the guy."

He handed the card to Claire. Dom leaned in to look at it over her shoulder. Neither one of them were surprised to see it was the business card of Melvin Blunt.

Chapter 10

Dom squinted at the noon sun as they emerged from the dim bar.

"We need to find out who this blonde stranger is," Claire said.

"And who the *she* he referred to is *and* what she started." Dom's thoughts drifted to Mae Biddeford. She had motive—Blunt wanted to take her land *and* he played dirty, so he'd probably threatened her or pulled some shenanigans to get his way. But what could she have started that the stranger would finish? And how did Mae know the stranger? His words implied they had some sort of history. Dom thought Mae was a long shot. She would not have the physical strength to kill Blunt … unless, of course, she had a much younger and stronger accomplice.

"Boy, I'd feel a lot better if the killer was this stranger," Claire said as they headed toward the dock.

Dom wanted to think it was the stranger, too. His earlier fears of Sarah being involved had resurfaced when Emile had mentioned that Shane was the only sober one in the bar and that he'd driven Bob home. Dom couldn't figure out why that had blipped on his radar, though. Why did he think it unusual that Shane would be in the bar sober? He was probably just being paranoid. "Me, too, but we have to check all the suspects to be thorough."

"I think we need to pay a visit to the *Gull View Inn* and see what we can find out about the stranger," Claire said.

"I agree." Dom craned his neck toward the end of the long dock where the tour boats parked. "But first we can question two of our other suspects. I think I see Donovan down there. Maybe he and Bob are in."

They started down the dock. Dom noticed the wooden boards were unusually littered with bird poop and a strange, purple stain. "They need to clean this dock up."

"Uh-huh." Claire picked up the pace beside him. Dom could have sworn she was avoiding even looking at the dock. He shrugged and quickened his step to keep up with her.

Donovan's fishing charter had just come in. On board, the deck hand was gutting and cleaning the morning's catch of haddock. Dom was surprised at the way his stomach soured at the pungent, fishy smell. He'd smelled much worse at crime scenes, but the years away from the field had softened him. He took a deep breath as if taking in more of the fish smell could harden him back up.

Beside him, Claire seemed unaffected by the odor. "Hey, Donovan." She waved at Donovan, who was just coming out of the pilot house.

Dom couldn't help but glance at the twine net piled in the back of the boat. It was all blue.

Donovan came over to the boarding ramp and leaned against the boat railing. "You guys are back again? More questions?"

Dom shrugged sheepishly. "I guess so. We're just trying to figure this thing out and we got some interesting information."

"What's that?"

The last customer squeezed by Donovan with his gutted fish in a plastic bag. Donovan, Dom and Claire moved out of the way while the deckhand started spraying down the boat. Donovan side-stepped so as not to get hit by the spray, but he was a little slow. The deck hand grimaced as the spray splashed Donovan's scuffed boat shoes and the bottom of his tan Dockers, wetting the bottom inch and soaking into a faint grease smudge on the inside cuff.

"Sorry, boss," the deckhand said.

Donovan laughed it off and waved to the deck hand to continue. "No worries. They need to be cleaned anyway." He turned to Dom and Claire. "You wouldn't believe how much time I spend doing laundry. Now, what were you saying about something interesting?"

"Oh, right," Dom continued, watching Donovan's face carefully. "We heard the murder victim, Milton

Blunt, was going to open a tour boat business just like yours."

Donovan studied the deck of his boat, then his eyes drifted across the long planks of the dock to where Barnacle Bob's boats bobbed up and down. "So, that's why he was so upset."

"He?" Claire asked. "You mean Bob Cleary? What makes you say he was upset."

Donovan snapped his attention back to Claire. "Oh, nothing. I mean, I knew he was out of sorts because of the divorce and all, and he did mention something about another boat cruise outfit the other night, but I thought he was just babbling. So, that was true? Someone really is going to start another boat charter?"

"Was," Dom said. "According to Josie, Blunt signed papers to rent the long dock just the other day."

"Well, I'll be. I guess Molly must have known about it, seeing as she works with Josie. Maybe that's how Bob found out."

"Maybe." Dom studied Donovan. "You didn't know about it, then?"

Donovan shook his head. "No."

"You were at *Duffy's* Friday night, right?" Claire asked.

"Yep."

"Did you notice Blunt there having words with anyone?"

Donovan's face turned sheepish. "I can't say that I did. I have to admit I had a bit too much to drink."

Dom's brow drifted up. "Really? Were you drinking with Bob?"

Donovan shook his head. "No. We aren't that good friends. But I saw him there. He was feeling pretty good himself."

"Did you see who was buying Bob drinks or notice when he left?"

Donovan's brow creased. "Buying him drinks? I wouldn't know about that, but I think he was still there when I left at around ten."

"Did you go straight home?"

"No. Like I said, I had a few too many and I didn't want to drive. I live on the other side of town. So I walked to my sister Sally's over on Packard Road. It's only a mile or so. I stayed there overnight. She doesn't mind me sleeping on the couch, but I won't do that again."

"Why not?"

Donovan grinned. "I woke up to my nephew Jonathan jumping up and down on the couch to get me up. Not what you want when you've been drinking. Sally did make me breakfast, though, so I guess I can't complain."

"Did you notice Blunt arguing with a stranger?"

Donovan's cheek moved in and out while he thought about the question. "I didn't pay much attention to Blunt and the bar was full. Lots of strangers were in there. The Crab Festival brings them in. Why do you ask? You think this stranger killed Blunt?"

"Maybe. We're just trying to cover all the angles." Dom's attention moved across the dock to Barnacle Bob's fleet. "Do you now if Bob Cleary is around?"

Donovan looked at his watch. "No, his charter doesn't come in for another hour."

"Oh. Well, I guess we can talk to him later, then."

Dom raised a brow at Claire in an unspoken question as to whether she had anything else to ask.

"Nice talking to you, Donovan." Apparently she was done questioning him, too, because she turned and led the way down the dock.

"That wasn't all that informative," she said once they were out of hearing distance.

"I don't know about that. I found it interesting that Bob knew about Blunt's boat charter venture. He had to know that would impact his business and that gives him a motive."

"True, but if he was as stumbling drunk as he said he was, I doubt he had the ability to strangle Blunt and dump him in the pot," Claire pointed out.

"Sure, but maybe he wasn't as drunk as everyone says."

"Like the Beauchamp case." Claire referred to one of their cases in Boston where the killer had gone to great pains to put on a show of how wasted he was at a party so that later on everyone would testify that he wouldn't have been physically able to murder someone.

Dom thought it was a long shot, but everything had to be considered. "No one saw who was buying him drinks. Maybe he made that up to make it *seem* like he drank a lot and didn't realize it. It's easy enough to act drunk in a bar full of people drinking."

Claire gnawed her bottom lip. "Emile said Shane drove Bob home. Maybe he noticed something. But I hate to think that was the case. I just kind of assumed Blunt pissed someone off and was killed on the spur of the moment."

"But if Bob faked being drunk so he could give himself an alibi, that means Blunt's death was premeditated murder."

Chapter 11

The *Gull View Inn* was a short walk from the docks, so Dom and Claire headed there next. As they huffed up the steep hill toward the Victorian-style bed and breakfast, Dom said, "At least we can cross one person off our suspect list."

"You mean Donovan?" Claire asked.

"Yes. It would seem he has an alibi if went to his sister's at ten. Unless he wasn't telling the truth."

Claire thought about that. She'd been watching Donovan carefully during their conversation and she hadn't noticed any body language to indicate he was lying. Not only that, but she could tell by the open-faced grin that spread on his face when he talked about his nephew that he adored the boy, which made him an even less likely suspect in her book. "It will be easy enough to find out if he was lying. We can just ask Sally. And we also need to talk to Bob Cleary again in person, given what we just discovered."

Dom nodded. "Did you get any indication he had something to hide when you talked to him before? How did he sound?"

"He sounded hungover. Not guilty of anything. But he did say he didn't remember what happened that night. I guess he could have drunk enough that he blacked out and didn't remember, so then he wouldn't have any guilty feelings." Claire tilted her head and gazed out at the slice of blue ocean that appeared between two houses. "But if he was that drunk, you would think Blunt would've been able to ward him off. Strangling someone takes strength and I would think it would be pretty hard if you were drunk."

"I was thinking that, too. Maybe Bob had some help or maybe Blunt was drunk or incapacitated in some way," Dom said as he opened the latch on the white picket fence and gestured for Claire to precede him up the flower-lined brick walkway.

Claire had a hard time believing it was Bob, and she hated to think another islander, also probably a friend of hers, had helped him. Then again, she was glad that Dom hadn't mentioned that Mae and Tom had motives, so she figured she'd let this line of questioning play out. She was still rooting for the mysterious stranger.

They ascended the steps to the wide porch. Claire paused for a moment to take in the fantastic view of the Atlantic Ocean that peeked at her from between lush, pink roses that trailed along the porch railings. Set on the hill, the *Gull View Inn* had been a bed and breakfast for over one hundred years. It had been handed down through several generations to the current owner, an elderly spinster named Velma who now ran it with her friend, Hazel.

They opened the front door and stepped into the lobby, which boasted a honey-colored, ornate woodwork stairway that matched the polished, wide-board floors. The stairway was rounded and a heavy, oak semi-circular reception desk that followed the shape of the stairs sat directly across from them. The air was spiced with the scent of lemons and roses.

Velma looked up at them from behind the desk where she was bending over the guest register.

"Hi, Claire and Dom. What brings you here? Surely you don't need a room?" Velma joked.

Claire leaned across the desk and lowered her voice. "We have a question about one of your guests."

Velma's thin, snow-white brows quirked up with interest. "Really? That sounds juicy." She slipped out from behind the desk and, in an exaggerated motion, glanced around furtively to make sure no one was watching. She jerked her snow-white bun toward a door marked private and tiptoed over, opening the door and gesturing for Claire and Dom to enter.

The room was a spacious office overlooking the large back deck which was an extended part of the *Gull View Inn* restaurant. Dozens of round tables ringed with blue-cushioned chairs and shaded by colorful, blue and white striped umbrellas dotted the deck. It was past the lunch hour, but some patrons lingered over their meals, enjoying the view of the harbor. Claire's stomach growled.

Velma indicated for them to sit on a pair of delicate, needlepoint chairs. Dom eyed the chairs dubiously. Claire figured he was wondering if the chair would break when he sat in it because she was actually wondering the same thing. She perched on the edge of the seat cautiously.

Velma leaned her thin hip on the corner of a mahogany partner's desk. "Now tell me, is this part of the murder investigation?"

"Sort of," Claire hedged. She didn't want to alarm Velma that a murderer might be staying at her inn, although she had the suspicion the older woman would find it more intriguing than alarming. "The victim was seen fighting with a blond man and someone said they thought he might be a guest here."

Velma slipped off the edge of the desk and went around to the other side. Opening a red leather book, she flipped to a page in the middle and ran her index finger down the length of the paper. "Oh, yes, that's right we do have a blond-haired man here. Mr. Naughton. A young guy, right?"

"That's right." Dom inched forward in his chair. "Is he still here?"

Velma's finger slid over to the right. "Yes. He's still here. But he couldn't be involved in the murder. He's such a nice young man." She indicated a dainty, blue-flowered porcelain candy dish filled with what looked like acorns. "See, he brought us these caramel root beer acorns from the *Harbor Fudge Shop*. Said they were his favorites and they are quite tasty."

Velma plucked an acorn out of the dish and popped it into her mouth as if to prove the point.

Claire didn't think the combination of root beer and caramel sounded tasty at all, and it certainly didn't mean that Mr. Naughton wasn't a killer. They'd put quite a few 'nice young men' who gave old ladies candy in jail for murder in their day. They both knew that most killers didn't go around acting mean and nasty. In fact, many of them hid behind a façade of nicety.

"Do you know what time he came in the night before last?" Claire asked.

Velma's cheek puffed out as she transferred the acorn candy there so she could answer.

"You mean the night of the murder?" She paused, swishing the candy around in her mouth as she thought about it. "I'm not sure. He ate dinner here. We had Hazel's famous beef stew. And then he went out … but I don't know when he came back. We go to bed at nine sharp and leave a key under the mat for those who come in later. He wasn't back when we turned in at nine."

Dom patted his left eyebrow. "Do you happen to know why he's here? Is he alone?"

Many people came to the island on vacation, especially when there was an event like the Crab Festival, but they usually didn't come alone. If the stranger was here alone, that would seem to indicate his business was not that of a vacation. Then again, if he was the killer, why would he still be here?

"He *is* alone at the hotel." Velma's lips puckered as she sucked on the candy. "But I don't think he plans to be alone for long. And I doubt he is your killer. It seems he might be here to court a young lady." Her eyes sparkled with the thought of young love.

Claire smiled at the old-fashioned notion. "Really? What makes you say that?"

"Well, late last night I couldn't sleep." She leaned forward and lowered her voice. "Don't tell Hazel, but her chicken gumbo gives me heartburn. Anyway, I got up to take some Maalox and I happened to see him in the rose garden with someone."

Claire leaned forward in her chair, her full attention on Velma. A suspicious, mysterious stranger having a clandestine meeting in the middle of the night? Sounded like suspect material to her.

"Who was it? What did she look like?" Claire asked.

"Did you hear what they were saying?" Dom added.

Velma straightened. "I don't know who it was. I'm not in the habit of eavesdropping on my guests. I only looked out for a second and the bushes were in the way, but by the way they had their heads bent together and the urgent whispering, I could tell that they must have had something very important to discuss."

Chapter 12

"Who do you think the stranger was meeting with?" Claire asked in hushed tones as they retreated down the brick walkway toward the street.

Dom's brows itched. This new development was interesting, but there was no evidence indicating the stranger was meeting with someone about Blunt. "I have no idea. We need to look into this Mr. Naughton."

"Indeed. And let's not forget that Shane drove Bob Cleary home. Bob and Naughton are high on my suspect list."

"Surely you don't think Shane had something to do with the murder?" Thinking of Shane gave way to thoughts of Sarah and the twine behind her counter. All circumstantial, but uncomfortable thoughts, nonetheless. Dom glanced over at Claire. A pang of guilt gnawed at him for not telling her about the argument he'd seen between Sarah and Blunt.

He had a gut feeling that Sarah was no killer, but since when did he let gut feelings figure into his cases? He operated on logic and physical evidence. Maybe he'd been hanging around with Claire too much.

"The stranger could have been meeting with anyone," Dom pointed out.

"Velma said it was a woman," Claire said.

"She said she *thought* it was a woman," Dom corrected her. "But her eyesight is not that great and she could only hear whispers."

They paused at the white picket gate. "It would make sense if the person he was meeting was a woman, especially in light of the fact that he was heard telling Blunt he would 'finish what *she* started.'"

"You think the woman he met with is this mysterious *she*? Looks like we need to figure out who she is. It could be someone from the island." Dom lifted the gate latch and swung the gate open, his thoughts turning to their one female suspect—Mae Biddeford. Could she be connected to Naughton in some way? Perhaps he was a nephew. But if so, wouldn't Claire and Velma recognize him?

Squeak. Squeak-ity. Squeak.

"What is that?"

Dom turned in the direction of the noise to see Jonathan Kimmel peddling in their direction on a sparkling green sting-ray. The bike was a little big for him, but judging by the grin on his face, he didn't mind.

"That's Donovan's nephew," Claire said. "We should

ask him if his uncle really did sleep over the night before last."

"Whoa, there." Dom stepped out into the boy's path. "Sounds like the chain on your bike is rubbing."

Jonathan stopped. Leaning to the side, he balanced on his right foot, looked down at the side of the bike and nodded. "It's been doing that for a few days. Uncle Donny fixed it for me, but it's started up again."

"Let me see," Dom said.

Jonathan kicked out the kick-stand and hopped off while Dom bent down and fiddled with the chain.

"I heard your uncle Donovan stayed over Friday night," Claire said.

Jonathan's face broke into a smile. "Yeah, Uncle Donny came over and surprised Momma. She wasn't very happy, but I was 'cause I got to stay up later since I was just about to go to bed when he came over."

"When is your bedtime?" Claire asked.

"It's usually nine o'clock," Jonathan grinned at Claire proudly. "But since it was Friday night, Mommy let me stay up an hour later to watch TV."

"So you got to stay up until ten, then?" Claire said as if it was the most scandalous revelation she'd heard all day.

Jonathan nodded.

"And your uncle was still there in the morning? I bet that was fun."

"Yep. I jumped on him and woke him up." Jonathan frowned. "He didn't like that as much as I thought he would."

Claire laughed. "I don't imagine he would."

Dom finished with the chain and stood up. "There. I think that ought to work. The screws that hold the chain guard were loose and the chain was rubbing. That should hold for a while, but the screws are almost stripped so I think your uncle needs to reattach the chain guard with new screws or it's gonna just keep happening."

"Thanks, mister!" Jonathan gave Dom a big smile, hopped on the bike and headed down the hill, leaving Dom looking at his grease-stained fingers.

"Looks like we can cross Donovan off our list," Claire said.

"Yeah, sounds like he really was at his sister's." Dom gladly accepted the napkin Claire had produced seemingly out of nowhere and he used it to wipe his fingers, methodically brushing the grease from each finger one at a time as they started back down the hill. "So that leaves Bob, Tom and Mae as our suspects."

"And the stranger," Claire added.

"Right. Let's not forget about him."

Claire sighed. "I'd like to think it was the stranger, but I have to admit it's not looking good for Bob."

"One big clue is the murder weapon. The twine. Who had access to that?" Dom tried not to think about the twine behind Sarah's counter.

Claire tried not to think about the twine around Mae's jam jars. "We could ask Marj down at the country store. I think anyone could buy it, but do you really think the murderer bought it special to kill Blunt with?"

"No. I doubt it. It was probably just something that was handy."

"And who had brown twine handy?"

"Bob."

They were three quarters of the way down the hill now and had a bird's-eye-view of the pier and dock. Claire looked over at the spot where Bob docked his fishing boat. It was empty. "Bob's still not back, so we can't talk to him. And besides, I just don't think it's in his nature to kill. *Anyone* could have grabbed twine off his boat. I saw that he keeps those nets unsecured in the back. It would be easy enough to reach in and grab some."

"True," Dom said. "But we need to go by the facts here, not supposition." He glanced at Claire out of the corner of his eye. "And not feelings."

Claire stiffened. "I think my *feelings* helped us with a few cases back in the day and besides, we don't really have any concrete clues to go on."

Dom sighed. "You have a point there. This is a lot harder than when we had access to police information. Maybe we should pay that visit to Robby."

"Maybe we won't have to." Claire nodded toward the dock where she'd been watching Robby come off Donovan's boat. He had his head down. His police cap hid the expression on his face, but the way he was walking so purposefully down the dock indicated he was deep in thought.

They picked up speed, but weren't quick enough to intercept him before he reached the end of the dock and turned in the opposite direction.

Claire jogged toward him. "Robby? Robby!"

Robby spun around, apparently surprised to see his aunt running after him. The manila folder slipped from his hand. Photographs scattered all over the dock.

Claire and Dom bent to help pick them up. Dom froze when he recognized what they were—photographs of the giant crab boil pot and the dirt area around it. The crime scene.

Claire must have noticed, too, because she slowed her normally quick movements, purposely taking her time picking up the photographs so she could study them, just like Dom was doing.

The first thing he noticed was a lot of footsteps in the dirt. There were many different types of shoe prints. He knew one of those must be of Blunt's killer. The others were of Blunt and whoever had walked over there in between the murder and the time the police closed the area down. With a start, Dom recognized his own shoe print and he realized some of those prints would be his and the other committee members—they'd walked all over the area before the police had come.

One photograph stood out from the others. This one had the usual footprints, but there was one clear area where no footprints had fallen. It was in an unusual shape that Dom couldn't quite make out, but that looked almost like part of a crab claw holding something long and jagged.

It wasn't really the shape that struck him. It was the fact that no footprints were on *top* of the shape. Someone had picked that item up after everyone came on the scene and before the police started taking pictures. Dom's eyebrows tingled … he was sure that what he was looking at was a clue.

Robby grabbed the pictures from them and shoved

them in the manila folder. They all stood up. "Hi, Auntie. What are you doing here?"

"We were just out for a stroll. What are *you* doing here?" Claire asked. "Something to do with the case?"

"I was interviewing Donovan. I guess it's no secret the victim was opening a tour boat operation."

"We heard that," Dom said. "Seems like he had a lot of things going on that would hurt businesses and people on the island."

"He did, but I hate to think that one of *us* would have killed him because of that." Robby looked over Dom's shoulder at the Atlantic. "Although he did pull some nasty tricks to get what he wanted like the tricks he pulled on Mae."

Claire's brows tugged together. "What do you mean 'what he pulled on Mae'?"

Robby blanched. "Oh, I guess I probably shouldn't have said anything."

Claire gave her nephew a stern look. "Come on, now. You can't leave us hanging or we'll imagine all sorts of things."

"Okay," Robby said. "I guess it's not a secret anyway and you could find out from Mae, but Blunt ratted her out to the health inspector. Blunt seemed positive her kitchen where she makes the jam wouldn't pass inspection."

"Did Mae know this?" Claire asked.

Robby nodded. "She must have known. She had the inspection yesterday morning."

Dom's brows went into tingling overdrive. He turned to Claire. "That must have been why she was late to the

Crab Festival committee meeting on the dock."

"Yeah, but it's odd that she didn't mention it or that she knew Blunt." Claire chewed her lip nervously.

"Unfortunately, that's what Zambuco thinks, too," Robby said. "He said something about how Blunt unleashing the inspector on her would put a dampener on her little jam business and *that* gives her a compelling motive in his book."

"That's ridiculous. Mae isn't much taller than five feet. She wouldn't be able to reach up and strangle a big guy like Blunt," Claire pointed out.

"Sure, she wouldn't be tall enough to strangle him when he was standing, but Blunt wasn't strangled when he was standing."

Dom's eyes widened. "What? What do you mean he wasn't standing?"

"He was hit on the head pretty hard with something heavy, knocked unconscious and *then* strangled. He was lying on the ground, so even a person of Mae's short stature could have done that by herself … but Zambuco said he wouldn't be surprised if she had a little help."

Chapter 13

Claire sat in the uncomfortable passenger seat of Dom's Smart Car, her lips pressed tightly together thinking of Mae Biddeford. She'd known Mae her whole life. Sure, Mae could be abrasive at times, but Claire doubted the woman—who tirelessly collected money for the local church fund, handed out meals at the homeless shelter, and fostered dozens of cats and dogs while they awaited their forever home—was a killer.

"I'm sure Mae couldn't have done it." Claire watched the town whiz by, the buildings replaced by tall pines and oaks as they drove away from the cove to the center of the island and the Biddeford farm.

"I hate to think it could be her," Dom said. "But we can't ignore the evidence and motive."

"Evidence? What evidence?"

"I'm not sure exactly what Zambuco has. Maybe

something in those pictures of the crime scene Robby had in his hand."

"What did you make of those? It just looked like a lot of footprints to me," Claire said.

"There were footprints, but there was also one peculiarity."

"Oh?"

"There must have been something there on the ground when we were walking around the pot, before we discovered the body. In the photos there was an oddly shaped area that was devoid of footprints. But I saw our footprints all around it."

Leave it to Dom to pick up on a subtle clue like that. Claire suddenly was glad she'd teamed up with him. She would have missed that, but Dom was very good at putting together the physical evidence.

"So, we stepped on top of the item and that's why it's shape was imprinted in the dirt cleanly with no footprints over it," she mused. "What was it?"

Dom shrugged. "I have no idea. It looked like a crab claw holding something misshapen. Maybe some kind of sign or something. Does that ring a bell?"

Claire dredged through her memory banks. This being Crab Cove, there were plenty of signs and logos that featured crab claws. She didn't remember one holding something misshapen, though. "No. But the police must have it, so maybe we can find out."

"That's just the thing, I don't think they do have it. If they did, they would have taken a picture of the item, not just its impression."

Claire twisted in her seat and frowned at Dom. "That

can't be right because if our footprints were around it, that means it was there when we found the body. And if the police didn't take it, where did it go?"

Dom's sideways glance told her all she needed to know. There was only one answer—one of *them* had taken it.

"Mae couldn't have taken it. She wasn't there," Claire said.

"I know, but who *did* take it. Do you remember anyone picking something up?"

Claire shook her head. "If someone did, you would think they would have handed it over once they realized it was a crime scene. But maybe they just thought it was trash and tossed it out."

"I didn't see anyone toss anything out," Dom said.

"Well, I hardly think any one of the people on the committee killed him and then took it as evidence. I mean, neither you nor I did it, so that leaves Tom, Norma and Jane."

"Yeah, you're right. None of it makes sense. Maybe whatever it was has nothing to do with the murder."

"The killer could have picked it up before we got there," Claire suggested. "Or in between us discovering the body and the police coming."

"I don't think so. The object must have been there when we were inspecting the area, otherwise there would be footprints inside it. The footprints were only *outside* it. It would have been very odd if we all missed stepping on that one patch of dirt," Dom said. "And I don't remember anyone else going in after we found the body. We held them back until the police came."

Claire twisted her lips. "You're right. It doesn't make sense. Bob Cleary wasn't there, and he has a compelling motive and doesn't have an alibi. But let's not forget the stranger who threatened Blunt. He seems like a good bet to me, but I didn't notice a blond stranger that morning.

"It could also have been the mysterious woman Velma saw Naughton meeting with."

Claire wondered who the mystery woman was and hoped it was a stranger since their only female suspect was Mae. Her mind flashed to the argument she'd seen between Blunt and Mae and a pang of guilt stabbed through her. Dom and she were partners now and she *should* tell him, but she didn't want to make things look worse for Mae. Better to wait until they got something concrete to cross Mae off the suspect list.

"Well, I'm sure Mae didn't do it. I don't know why Zambuco is fixated on her when there are more interesting suspects. I'm sure Mae will be able to clear herself from suspicion when we talk to her," Claire said.

Dom turned down the dirt road that led to the Biddeford farm and slowed to a crawl.

Claire perched anxiously on her seat. She was in a hurry to get to Mae and prove her innocence before Zambuco did something stupid. "You can go thirty-five on this road."

"I know, but the dirt kicks up and I don't want to get my car dirty. I just washed it this morning."

Claire rolled her eyes. Dom was a little OCD when it came to his car, among other things. "You wash it every day."

Honk!

Claire looked in the side-view mirror to see a plume of dirt coming up behind them. She adjusted the mirror and recognized Norma in the beige golf cart she used to run about town. By the pace at which she was gaining on them, she must have had the pedal pushed to the floor.

"Get out'ta the way!" Norma made motions with her hand as if she intended to pass them, but Dom was already turning down the long driveway to the Biddeford farm.

"What's she in such a hurry for?" Dom asked as Norma sped past them on the dirt road, honking and waving.

"You know Norma. She has only one speed—impatient. She's probably going to Tom Landry's for goat cheese. It's her favorite." Claire could practically taste the tangy raw cheese that she also bought from Tom's farm. She remembered she was running low. "I need to stop there, myself."

The Biddeford farmhouse was a big, white, three-story with a peaked roof and a wide porch that ran along three sides. A two-level red barn sat across the driveway from the house and an old German Shepherd lounged lazily in the half open doorway of the barn. He lifted his head and sniffed the air as Claire and Dom got out of the car.

"Hey, Shep." Claire squatted beside the dog, scratching behind his ear. Shep phantom-scratched with his back leg and looked at her adoringly with his golden-brown eyes.

"Claire! What are you doing here?" Mae appeared on the porch wearing a white apron with small double cherries stamped all over it. The middle of the apron was stained bright red and Claire figured the stain was either raspberry or strawberry jam. Apparently, the health inspector had not shut Mae down as Blunt had hoped.

Claire stood and scuffed the dirt with her shoe. Dom moved away so the dry dirt wouldn't soil him. "We stopped by to talk to you about Blunt."

Mae's face hardened. "What about him?"

"Zambuco seems to think you would have motive to want him dead and we wanted to come out and see if we could help you," Dom said.

"We know you're innocent and we figure we have the experience to help you set Zambuco straight," Claire added.

Mae crossed her arms over her chest. "Why? What did Zambuco say to you?"

"We didn't actually talk to Zambuco, but Robby said Blunt tried to get the health inspector after you."

"That's right. The dirty so-and-so. He tried to set me up. Claimed he found goat hair in my jam." Mae's voice rose an indignant octave. "I guess he figured if my kitchen got shut down, I'd be out of business and willing to sell the farm to him."

"Did he pay the health inspector off or something?" Claire asked.

Mae shook her head. "No. He planted the hair and then I guess he probably planned to sabotage me somehow when the inspector was here, but Blunt never showed up and I passed the inspection."

"When was that?"

"Morning before yesterday, when Blunt was … well, you know."

Dom frowned at Mae. "You knew Blunt was planning to sabotage you?"

"Well, of course. I know there's no hairs in my jam. How would a goat hair even get in there? And my kitchen is spotless, so I'm sure he planned to slip something in there that morning when I wasn't looking. Somehow, he finagled an invitation to be in on the inspection."

Claire glanced toward Tom Landry's farm. There would be plenty of goat hair over there, but how would it get into Mae's kitchen? Was Blunt planning on using the goat hair against Tom, too? "Did you tell this to Zambuco?"

"Darn tootin' I did," Mae said proudly.

Claire's stomach pinched. No wonder Zambuco thought Mae was the killer. She'd even given him a reason to suspect her. Which, to Claire, proved more than anything that Mae didn't do it. If she *was* the killer, she certainly wouldn't have indicated to the police that she would have benefitted from making sure Blunt didn't show up for that inspection.

"That's why Zambuco has you high on the suspect list," Dom said.

Mae's face wrinkled in confusion. "Well, I don't see why Zambuco would suspect *me* because Blunt plays dirty."

"You told him you suspected Blunt was going to sabotage your kitchen for the inspection, right? Getting Blunt out of the way before the inspection would cause the inspection to go better for you. See why he would suspect you?"

Mae's mouth formed a small 'O'. "Gee, I didn't think of it that way."

"Is that why you were late to the Crab Festival meeting that morning?" Claire asked.

Mae nodded. "Yes. The inspector was coming earlier that morning. I would've made it to the meeting on time, except Blunt never showed for the inspection. The inspector waited a good half-hour for him, too."

"I suppose you were at home in bed asleep earlier that morning," Claire said.

Mae scowled at her. "Of course. Where else would I be? But I wasn't asleep. I was scouring the kitchen for the inspector. And it must have worked, because I passed with flying colors."

"So you can still make your jams." Claire's thoughts of Mae's jams turned to thoughts of the brown twine that had been wrapped around Blunt's neck. "Why didn't you say something about the inspection or that you knew who the victim was and even had an appointment with him that morning when we found Blunt at the Crab Festival?"

A crimson stain crept across Mae's cheeks. She looked down at her white tennis shoes. "I was embarrassed. I mean, I'm practically famous for my jams. I did win the *Crabby* last year, so how would it look if the cleanliness of my kitchen was brought into question?"

Dom's bushy brows mashed together. "The *Crabby*?"

Mae's blush deepened. "Yes, it's quite prestigious. Each year, it's awarded to one islander for excellence in their field. We've been doing it for about five years and I won last year."

Claire thought about her kitchen cupboard stuffed full of excess jars of Mae's jam. The truth was, her jams were quite tasty but she gave them out so frequently that most of the islanders had so many extra jars they'd be bequeathing them to relatives in their wills for generations to come. Claire remembered how proud Mae had been to win the odd trophy, which was a giant two-and-a-half foot tall monstrosity made out of silver-colored metal in the shape of a crab holding a silhouette of Mooseamuck Island.

"I can see you are quite proud of the award and your jams." Dom studied Mae as if he was trying to decide whether she was proud enough to kill someone over it.

Claire thought about Mae's new design with the brown twine. She couldn't really blame Dom for looking at her that way, but she also couldn't picture the senior citizen getting out of bed in the wee hours of the morning, sneaking down to the pier and strangling Blunt.

Claire looked out over Mae's farm. The strawberries were planted in neat rows in front of almost an acre of blueberry and raspberry bushes. Pear trees dotted the sides of the field and even the backyard of the farm, where white linen sheets flapped in the breeze on a clothesline strung between two massive oak trees. A pair of goldfinches twittered around a bird feeder filled with thistle.

Beyond the rows of strawberries, a cloud of dust rose in the air along the road that led to Tom's farm.

"Anyway, surely Zambuco can't be serious about

thinking I killed Blunt," Mae said. "He was a nasty piece of work, and I'm sure there are other people that wanted him dead more than I did."

The cloud of dust drew closer. Claire squinted into the distance just as a golf cart emerged from the dust. It was Norma, driving exceedingly fast, even for her. She started honking the cart's high-pitched horn and waving her cane in the air.

The commotion caught Dom and Mae's attention and they all stared as the cart careened into Mae's driveway, screeching to a stop in front of them. Norma's face was tight with anxiety and she swished her cane in the air like a sword.

"Hurry up and get in! Zambuco's at Tom's and I think he's fixing to arrest him!"

Chapter 14

Claire's tailbone slammed against the thinly cushioned rear seat of the golf cart as it sped toward Tom Landry's farm. Her mouth was dry from the dust that whipped up around the tires and swirled into her face. For once, she wished that Dom was driving, but Norma had insisted and somehow Dom had commandeered the front seat, leaving her and Mae riding backwards in the rear.

In Tom's field, she could see Zambuco, Robby and Tom standing near a log post fence. Norma whipped the cart in that direction and Claire's knuckles turned white as she grasped onto the metal safety bar to keep from being flung off. She reached out and grabbed the back of Mae's apron to keep her from sliding out. The cart screeched to a halt and the four of them jumped off.

Zambuco scowled at them. "What are you people doing here?"

"We're here to help Tom," Claire said. "What's going on?"

Zambuco pointed to a hole in the ground. "Your friend here had a motive to want Blunt dead. We heard he was in *Duffy's* the night Blunt was killed. We came up to ask a few questions and caught him burying the murder weapon."

Claire looked into the empty hole, her stomach sinking. Tom *did* have a motive. Blunt was trying to take his farm. And Emile had mentioned that Tom was in the bar that night. Tom had also been at the scene of the crime that morning with the Crab Festival committee. Claire remembered him dropping his clipboard. Had he dropped it on purpose so he could pick up a piece of evidence he'd left behind the night before?

"The murder weapon? What do you mean?" Norma demanded. "I thought Blunt was strangled."

"Bludgeoned *and* strangled," Zambuco said. "Technically, the strangling did him in."

Claire's eyes flicked up to Tom's face. She didn't see the face of a killer. She saw the face of a very scared and worried man. Tom's body language and demeanor was not like that of any murderer she'd caught so far. She was sure Tom wasn't the one. But if he wasn't, then why was he burying the murder weapon? Maybe what he was burying wasn't the murder weapon and this was all a mistake.

"We don't know if he did it alone. He might be in cahoots with your friend here." Zambuco nodded toward Mae.

"Well … well … well … I …" Mae huffed.

Norma snorted. "In cahoots? Why, the two of them have hardly said a nice word to each other in over seventy years. I doubt they'd combine forces now to kill somebody. And where is this supposed murder weapon, anyway?"

"It's not actually the whole murder weapon," Robby chimed in. "It's just part of it."

He held up a plastic bag that had a thick metal piece inside. It was silver in color and, if Claire wasn't mistaken, that dark stain on the jagged edge was blood. But was it Blunt's blood?

Robby turned the bag around to show the other side and something niggled in Claire's brain. The piece looked like the same shape of the imprint that had been found in the dirt by the crime scene—the crab claw holding something jagged. Claire now recognized what that jagged something was. It was part of the outline of Mooseamuck Island.

"What the heck is that?" Norma asked.

Mae gasped, and her wide eyes never left the bag as she said, "It's a *Crabby*. I have one right at my house."

***

Zambuco wanted to see Mae's *Crabby*, so they all headed over to Mae's house.

As they were getting out of their various cars and golf carts, a shiny, new Volvo pulled in. Claire was surprised to see Jane step out and hurry over.

Claire's eyes flicked from her friend to the car. For the past fifteen years, Jane had driven an old station wagon with wood-grained sides. It must have finally given out, but this new car seemed expensive for Jane's modest salary. It wasn't a Mercedes, or a BMW, but it *was* brand new. Then again, what did Claire know? Maybe Jane had been saving up, knowing that her wagon was on its last legs.

"What's this? Is the whole town going to show up now?" Zambuco's voice complained even though his face seemed to indicate he was happy to see Jane. "Do you people have some sort of a telepathic grapevine?"

"No," Jane said. "I happened to be driving to Tom's farm for some goat's milk and I noticed the commotion here. Naturally, I pulled in to see what was going on."

"New car?" Claire asked.

Jane waved her hand at the car dismissively. "My old clunker finally died and I had to get something. So what *is* going on?"

"We caught Mr. Landry here with part of the murder weapon. And then Ms. Biddeford claims she's got the rest of it," Zambuco said.

"I didn't say I had the *rest* of it," Mae corrected him. "I said I have *one like it*. The trophy that piece came from. But mine is intact. It's not the murder weapon."

Jane looked confused. "I don't understand. What was Tom doing with the murder weapon?"

Zambuco fidgeted impatiently. "Isn't it obvious? He's the murderer."

Jane scowled at Zambuco and Claire saw something pass across his face that reminded her of a child who had been reprimanded. Did he actually care what Jane thought?

Jane fisted her hands on her hips. "Now, listen here Frank. I've known Tom Landry all my life and he is no murderer. I don't know what other evidence you have, but I'm quite certain it's not enough to arrest him."

"That may be," Zambuco said. "If he *is* innocent, he will be proven as such. Right now, I need to follow this lead." He turned to Mae. "Now, Ms. Biddeford, let's see this *Crabby* that you claim to have."

"He was killed with a *Crabby*?" Jane's eyes went wide. "But there's only five of those."

Robby held up the plastic bag. "Four-and-a-half now because one of them is missing this piece."

"If there are only five of them, that should make tracking down where it came from easy, but for now I'd like to see the one that Ms. Biddeford claims is in her possession." Zambuco waved his thick hands towards Mae's house. "Would you be so kind as to show us where it is?"

Mae led them up on the porch, through the squeaky screen door with its layers of green paint and into her raspberry-scented kitchen. The farmhouse kitchen had never been renovated other than the new stainless steel appliances Mae had purchased two years ago. Even though most of the kitchen was over a hundred years old, it wasn't shabby or dilapidated. Like most frugal New Englanders, the Biddefords had kept everything in tip-top shape.

The pine cabinets were painted a pale, cheery yellow. The butcherblock countertops showed signs of loving use, but still glowed a honey brown. The original copper sink, polished in some spots and green with patina in others, shined under the double windows that overlooked the peach trees in the back. White, sheer curtains sucked in and out against the screen in the breeze from the open window.

Even though everything in the kitchen was old, it was neat as a pin and could have been featured in a decorator's magazine highlighting the new trend toward time-worn primitive antiques.

On the counter sat a line of small, clear mason jars, red and white checked print lids and the incriminating brown twine all cut into small sections.

Zambuco zeroed in on the twine. "Where did you get this?"

"Bob Cleary gave it to me," Mae said. "I wanted something that reflected the history of Crab Cove to put on my new jam jar designs. And what better than fishing twine? The fishermen use it for their nets."

Zambuco raised a thick brow at Robby. He stared at the twine a little bit more, then whirled around toward Mae. "So, where is this *Crabby* trophy?"

Mae gestured toward a small door at the other end of the kitchen.

"I put it in the basement. I don't have it on display. I mean, I know I make a killer jam, but I don't like to put on airs by showing off the trophy."

"I'll go down with her," Zambuco said to Robby, "to make sure she doesn't pull anything funny. You stay here with the suspect." Zambuco pierced Tom with a glare just in case there was any question as to who he meant by 'suspect'.

Mae disappeared through the small door and Zambuco followed, scuffing his head on the top when he forgot to duck. "Ouch."

Claire stifled a laugh.

They sat around the kitchen in uncomfortable silence while they listened to the sounds of rummaging coming from below. Tom pulled one of the red Naugahyde chairs out from the chrome and Formica table and sunk into it. He picked a candy out of his pocket, the cellophane crinkling as he unwrapped it. Just before he popped it into his mouth, Claire recognized it as one of the caramel root beer acorns. Everyone seemed to be eating those. Maybe she should try one. She doubted she would like it and couldn't help but wonder if it was any coincidence that two of their potential suspects ate the same unusual candy. Probably not, she decided, but still filed the information away for later use.

Robby leaned against the counter, the evidence bag dangling from his hand. Norma thumped her cane on the floor impatiently. Dom busied himself by arranging the jam jars in a perfect line, bending down so his eyes were even with the counter to make sure there was an equal amount of space between each jar and that they were all equidistant from the edge.

Finally, Mae came through the door, the giant trophy clutched in her hands triumphantly.

"See, mine's not broken. I told you I'm not the killer." She set the trophy down on the kitchen counter and plopped into a seat at the table next to Tom.

Zambuco emerged from the doorway, this time taking care to bend down so as not to hit his head.

"So, it wasn't Mae's trophy." Zambuco turned to Tom. "Then it must have been yours."

Norma nudged Zambuco with her cane. "Guess again, Sherlock. Tom doesn't have a *Crabby*."

"Really? Then how did he end up with that?" Zambuco pointed to the piece of metal in the plastic bag which Robby was now comparing to the top of Mae's *Crabby*. It was a perfect match, proving that what Tom had been burying *was* the top of one of the island's prestigious trophies.

Tom sighed. "I saw it that morning when we found the body in the crab boil pot. At first, I thought it was just a piece of trash, then I recognized that it was part of the *Crabby*. I knew Mae had one and I knew Blunt had been threatening her and … well … I just picked it up. I don't think Mae killed him, but I didn't want her to get into trouble if the police found it and suspected the worst."

Mae's eyes got all soft and gooey. Her hand slowly crept across the table and brushed against Tom's. "Thanks, Tom."

"But you have a motive," Zambuco persisted. "I heard Blunt wanted your land, too."

"That's right. He did want my farm and I think he was getting ready to pull a fast one. He was supposed to meet with the dairy inspector at my farm around three the day before, but he turned up late. The inspector couldn't wait so he left before Blunt showed. I don't know what Blunt had in mind, but the inspector gave me the okay, so it turned out all right for me. I never did find out why Blunt was late, but he was really mad the inspector didn't wait for him."

"He was late because of me," Mae mumbled, suddenly taking an interest in smoothing the wrinkles on the embroidered napkin that was in front of her on the table.

Tom's brows tugged together. "What do you mean that he was late because of you?"

"I overheard him talking to the dairy inspector that morning. I think he planned to put something in your goat milk to get you in trouble. Just like he was planning to sabotage my kitchen. He'd already planted goat hair in one of my jam jars and reported me to the health inspector. Anyway, I couldn't let him get away with it, so I just happened to intercept him on the way to your farm. I had to break a whole tote bag full of my jams to keep him. Then I had to yell and fight with him. I guess it worked if it made him miss the inspection." Mae glanced shyly at Tom.

Tom turned in his chair to face Mae and slid his hand over hers. "You did that for me?"

Mae nodded. "We can't have someone like him taking our family farms, can we?"

"No, siree. My grandaddy farmed this land by hand."

"Mine, too."

"I heard they tilled the soil together and helped each other build that stone wall that separates our properties."

"They used teamwork." Mae's wistful smile turned into a frown. "And then they got into that feud."

"What was that about anyway?" Tom asked.

Mae shrugged. "Darned if I know."

Mae peered up at Tom from under her lashes. "Maybe we should bury the hatchet?"

Tom's face broke into a grin. "I think that's a great idea."

"Enough of this lovey-dovey stuff," Zambuco broke in. "You two are still suspects. Where were you that night?"

"I was at home, alone," Mae said.

"I was at *Duffy's* bar, keeping my eye on Blunt because I knew he was up to no good. I was hoping to get something on him, but no luck. I went home at midnight and went to bed. Alone."

"So neither one of you has an alibi. You were both at the scene of the crime the next morning. One of you was seen trying to dispose of one of the murder weapons." Zambuco pointed to the plastic evidence bag, then turned and picked up a piece of the twine, letting it slide through his sausage fingers. "And one of you has the other murder weapon right in her kitchen."

Norma smacked Zambuco's wrist with her cane and he jerked his hand back, his thick brows hooding dark, beady eyes that scowled at Norma.

"That's preposterous," Norma said. "That little piece you saw Tom trying to dispose of couldn't hurt a fly and anyone can get that twine from the fishing boats down at the dock."

"That's actually not true," Mae grimaced. "You can't get it in a long strand from the boats because it's netted. Bob had some for his net repair and he gave me a little of it, but he doesn't keep that on the boat."

"Mae's right. The twine is not that easy to come by," Robby said. "We checked."

"But the fishermen have it, and Blunt was also going to open a business that threatened their livelihood," Claire pointed out, then felt a pang of guilt. She'd just pointed the finger at Bob Cleary and she didn't want it to be him. But if she had to choose between him and Mae or Tom, she'd pick Mae and Tom every time.

Jane's brow creased. "He was?"

"Yes, he was opening a tour boat business that would compete with Barnacle Bob's and *Crabby* Tours."

"Pffft." Norma thumped her cane on the floor. "I've known Bob Cleary and Donovan Hicks since they were in diapers. They're not killers. It sounds to me like Blunt was a jerk. He probably made a lot of enemies wherever he went. I don't know why you're so keen to pin this on someone from Mooseamuck Island when it could easily be any one of the thousands of tourists that have flocked here."

"That's right. There was actually some stranger in the bar that had a big fight with Blunt the night he died," Tom said.

"Really? You wouldn't be just saying that to take the heat off you and Ms. Biddeford now, would you?" Zambuco looked like he thought Tom might be making it up.

"It's true," Claire chimed in, earning a pinch-faced look from Zambuco.

"You were there?" Zambuco asked her.

"Well, no. But we ... umm ... I happened to hear about it later," Claire said.

"I'm not as dumb as you people think," Zambuco said. "*Duffy's* was the last place the victim was seen, so naturally I asked around. I found out about the stranger and located him at the *Gull View Inn*. I have someone looking into him right now. But, that doesn't mean I can ignore the evidence in front of my face. I may have to pull the two of you in."

Mae's face registered alarm. "Pull us in? You mean arrest us?"

"Maybe"

Jane put her hand gently on Zambuco's arm. "Now, Frank. There's no need for that."

Zambuco frowned down at Jane, but Claire could see his face softening as their eyes met.

"They could be a flight risk," he said.

"They aren't. They have ties to the island. They grew up here. All their friends are here," Jane reasoned.

"Not to mention that neither one of them killed anyone," Norma added.

"Okay, fine. I have some other avenues to investigate, but my boss on the mainland is pressuring me to tie this one up and in twenty-four hours I'm going to have to hand him the name of the killer, or at least a viable suspect, so you *islanders* better get your crabs in a row." Zambuco pierced each one of them, except Jane, with a steely glare, turned on his heel and walked out, fumbling with the screen door which he practically ripped off the hinges.

Robby shot them an apologetic look and raced after him.

Claire glanced at Jane. It was rather disturbing that she kept calling Zambuco by his first name and the two of them seemed to be awfully familiar with each other. Not for the first time, Claire had the fleeting thought that there might be some interest between them, then dismissed it as preposterous. Zambuco was annoying and unkempt. Jane kept herself trim and was still very attractive. Claire was sure her friend could do much better than Frank Zambuco, even if he was more than a decade her junior.

Claire didn't know what was going on between Jane and Zambuco, but whatever it was she felt grateful. Jane had bought them some time to keep Mae and Tom out of jail and find the real killer. Claire just hoped she could pull it off before the twenty-four hours was up.

Chapter 15

"You don't think it really could be Mae or Tom, do you?" Dom asked Claire once they were back in the Smart Car and heading toward the docks.

"Of course not." Claire craned her neck to stare at the display of her phone which she was holding out the window. "I'm betting on this Naughton guy."

"But if it was him, why would he still be here on Mooseamuck Island?" Dom's eyebrow twitched. The only reason he could think of was that he had a tie with someone on the island. His accomplice.

Dom didn't want to think that Mae or Tom could have killed Blunt, but the truth was they both had a strong motive. And even though Mae still had her *Crabby*, that didn't mean they couldn't have used someone else's. In fact, it would be pretty clever of them if they did. "Who else has one of those *Crabbies*?"

Claire pressed her lips together as she angled the

phone to the right. "Well, let's see. There's Mae, Sally Kimmel, Norma, Bob Cleary and Velma at the *Gull View*."

"Bob Cleary has one?"

"Yes, I know what you're thinking. Bob is one of our suspects and he had access to the twine and the *Crabby*, but the *Crabby* at the *Gull View Inn* is on display right in the dining room on the mantle."

"So anyone could grab it …" Dom's voice trailed off.

"Yes, and we both know who is staying at the *Gull View* and would have easy access."

"Naughton."

"Yep. I'm trying to do a Google search right now and see if I can tie Blunt to Naughton somehow. We already know they have a history." Claire tsked at the phone display. "But the reception is so spotty here, it's taking forever."

"Even if he is involved, I think there must have been another person," Dom said. "There's no way one person could have gotten Blunt into that crab pot."

"Maybe Blunt got into the pot on his own while he was still alive and then got strangled inside," Claire suggested.

Dom slid her a sideways glance. Was she for real? "Why would he do that?"

Claire shrugged. "Who knows? We've seen stranger things happen. But let's say he did have help. Who do *you* think it was?"

"I guess we need to figure that out." Dom glanced down the long dock as he pulled into a parking spot near the pier. "It looks like Bob is on his boat. Maybe he'll say something that eliminates him as a suspect."

"Or incriminates him."

Claire fiddled with her phone all the way down the dock. A few times, she strayed too far toward the edge and Dom had to remind her to watch where she was going. He didn't know why she was bothering with the phone. Cell phone reception on the island was spotty at best and everyone knew it was the worst down by the docks.

Bob spotted them coming toward him and raised his hand in reply to Dom's greeting, then jumped off his boat and met them on the dock.

"Are you guys here with questions about Blunt?" Bob busied himself by running a white rag along the railing of his boat. Dom wondered if he was avoiding looking them in the face—then again, maybe he was just making good use of his time.

"Yes." Claire slipped her phone into her pocket and got straight to the point. "We were wondering if you knew that he was going to open a boat tour operation like yours."

Bob stopped polishing and looked at them. "Yes. We've known that for a few months, since the beginning of the season."

"We?" Dom asked.

"Me and Donovan. Funny thing is, that was the only thing we ever agreed on." Bob chuckled. "It kind of brought us together, in a way."

"So you talked about it?" Claire asked. "Donovan didn't give us the impression he knew it was a definite."

Bob screwed up his face. "Well, I thought he did.

We didn't talk too much. I mean, it's not like we're going to be best buddies overnight. Maybe he didn't give it as much credence as I did, but Molly tipped me off about it and it sounded like it was going to go through."

"Did you and Donovan talk about it in the bar?" Dom asked.

"I think we did, now that you mention it. That whole night is still fuzzy," Bob said.

"Was that why you were drinking so much? I mean, another tour boat company would really cut into your business," Claire said.

"It would, but I wasn't too worried. We're established and have customers that come back year after year. They bring their kids and then those kids grow up and bring *their* kids."

"That's right. Your business is highly regarded," Dom said. "Didn't you even win one of those awards?" Dom turned to Claire. "What is it called?"

"The *Crabby*."

Bob smiled proudly. "I did, actually. Three years ago."

"So you have one of those big trophies?" By the way Bob was acting, it appeared he had no idea Blunt had been knocked out with a *Crabby*. Either that or he was very confident that the police did not know about it.

"Yep. Keep it in the china cabinet, right next to Grandma Cleary's good china," Bob said proudly. "Anyway, like I told you, I wasn't intending to drink so much in the bar that night. If you're thinking I was angry or drowning my sorrows, that's not the case at all. Someone else was feeding me those drinks and they packed a wallop."

"Who?"

"That's the strange thing. I have no idea. I asked around and so far no one claims to have bought them."

No one had admitted it to Dom and Claire, either. Dom wondered if Bob was telling the truth. Why would someone buy him drinks and then not take the credit for it? That was totally out of character for the usually frugal Maine islanders. "Do you remember anything at all about Blunt that night in the bar?"

"Not really. I remember he was there. I don't like him much so I pretty much avoided him. He was at the bar and I took a table in the corner. I didn't talk to him ... at least, not from what I remember."

"But you said you don't remember much," Dom pointed out. "How do you know you didn't talk to Blunt?"

Bob grimaced. "I remember the early part of the night and during the parts I can't remember, I think I was too drunk to talk to anyone."

"Did Shane McDonough drive you home?" Claire asked.

Bob nodded. "Yes, I do remember that. I was too drunk to walk, never mind drive. Shane got me home and helped me get into the house. I remember because I had to give him a talking to about that girl of his."

"What do you mean?"

"She called him up and they were having a bit of a fight. You know, being newly divorced I'm a little sensitive to that sort of thing. I had to tell him to stop."

"Stop what?"

"He was telling her not to do something. Begging

her, really. Said she was making a big mistake and she'd regret it." Bob shook his head. "I told him to let her do what she wants. Happy wife, happy life. Even though they aren't married yet, you can't start too soon."

Dom felt a rock form in the pit of his stomach. Sarah fought with Blunt, then lied about knowing him and she had the brown twine. She didn't have a *Crabby*, but as Claire had pointed out, it wouldn't be impossible to get one. "Do you have any idea what it was she was planning on doing?"

"No, but whatever it was, Shane rushed off in a hurry to stop her from doing it."

Chapter 16

"Shane is doing a kitchen renovation over at the Ditmeyers. I think we should go straight there and talk to him." Claire squinted at her phone display, tilting it so as to reduce the glare from the sun.

"You don't think his fight with Sarah had anything to do with this, do you?" Dom kept his eyes on the road.

Claire slid her eyes from her phone to Dom. "I mostly wanted to ask him about how drunk Bob was that night and if Shane saw anything unusual in the bar. Do you think his fight with Sarah has something to do with Blunt?"

"Oh, I don't know. Probably not. Probably just one of those spats young couples get into. You know how volatile young relationships are."

Claire laughed. She did know how volatile relationships could be, but now that Dom mentioned it, the timing was coincidental. If Shane had rushed off after he dropped Bob, that would have been a few hours before Blunt was killed.

She gave herself a mental head shake—was she so desperate to prove it was not Mae or Tom that she would grasp at any straw? It was ridiculous to think Shane and Sarah had anything to do with it. For one thing, they had no motive.

The Ditmeyers had a small but neat cottage halfway up Israel Head Hill on the backside of the Island. Claire looked across the sapphire blue ocean as they pulled in. On a clear day, you could see all the way to the mainland, but today was a bit hazy.

"Oh, good. He's here." Claire pointed to Shane's truck and put her phone down on the dashboard. They both got out and started to pick their way across the lumber and tools lying around the yard.

Shane came out the front door and hesitated, with a look of surprise on his face when he saw them.

"Hi, Shane," Claire said.

"Hi." Shane switched his gaze from Claire to Dom. "The Ditmeyers aren't home."

"Actually, we came to talk to you," Dom said.

Shane's dark brows ticked up a notch. "Oh? What's up?"

"We wanted to ask you something about the other night. The night of the murder," Claire said.

Shane stuffed his hands in the pockets of his cargo shorts and squared his shoulders. "Sure, but I don't know anything about the guy who was killed."

"We know, but we heard you were in *Duffy's* that

night and drove Bob Cleary home."

"That's right."

"Blunt, the guy who was killed, was in the bar, too."

Shane rasped his right hand across the stubble on his chin. "Which one was he? There were a few non-islanders there that night, as I recall."

"He was a tall, lanky guy sitting at the bar."

"Oh, the one shouting obscenities at the Yankees?"

Claire remembered Floyd saying they were all jeering the Yankees that night. "I think that was him."

"I saw him there. What about him?"

"Did you see anyone arguing with him or notice anything strange?"

"Not really."

"What time did you drive Bob home?" Dom asked.

"Oh, about midnight."

Claire searched her memory banks. The stranger must have fought with Blunt before midnight because the ball game was still on. Wouldn't Shane have seen that? Maybe he was in the bathroom or just on the other side of the bar. *Duffy's* was a decent size and if it was a rowdy night, he might not have noticed a fight on the other side. And anyway, why would Shane lie?

"Was Bob really that drunk?" Dom asked.

"He was, but I pumped some coffee into him before we left and he seemed to be sobering up by the time I got him home."

"Did he mention that he was upset or mad about anything?" Claire asked.

Shane shook his head. "No. He didn't really seem upset. He seemed kind of anxious or excited actually.

He was in a hurry to get home. I helped him inside but he couldn't get rid of me fast enough."

"And what did you do after you dropped him off?" Claire said.

"Me?" Shane shifted his eyes to look out over the ocean. "I drove straight home and went to bed."

***

The cell phone slid across the dashboard as Dom pulled out of the Ditmeyers' driveway. Claire lunged for it, catching it before it spilled off onto her lap.

Dom thought about the next logical step. He realized Claire would probably want to do something based on her intuition and he didn't like the way she'd been interrogating Shane or the way she was glancing at him in her side-view mirror. Following Shane's trail might lead to Sarah and Dom felt that it would be better to follow the clues logically. If Sarah and Shane were involved, it would be exposed in the process.

"I think we need to account for every one of the *Crabby*'s," Dom said.

"Good idea." Claire focused on the phone. "Finally, I'm getting something on this darn thing."

"We can easily check out the one at the *Gull View Inn*, but some of the others might not be so easy. I say we start with Bob Cleary's since he's a suspect with motive and access to the twine."

"Okay." Claire slid her index finger down the length of her phone, her eyes never leaving the display. "That makes sense because it might clear Bob if it's in there … but if it isn't, it could incriminate two people."

"Two?"

"Bob and Shane. Shane had access to Bob's house when he dropped him off and I think Shane just lied to us about where he went afterwards."

Dom pursed his lips. She was right. But if Shane did have something to do with Blunt's death, that didn't necessarily mean Sarah was in on it. Either way, he was determined to uncover the truth. Better that he and Claire find out before Zambuco, even if it did turn out that Sarah was involved.

"How will we get into Bob's house, though? He's on his boat and I thought he lived alone," Dom said.

"He does, but he said he keeps the trophy in his china cabinet and I happen to know his dining room has big windows. We can just creep around back and peek in." Claire glanced up at Dom with a sneaky smile. "I know it's not what we would do if we were officially on the case, but we aren't official and we need to be a little more creative if we want to figure out who the killer is."

Dom was surprised to find that he liked the idea of being creative. It was refreshing not to be tied to police procedures, and since they didn't have the benefit of being official police consultants, they needed to gain an edge somehow.

A feeling of excitement surged through him. He'd been worried about solving the case, but somehow this realization made him feel like he now had the tools to do just that. Dom had never done anything that wasn't to police protocol before, but now his mind wondered what other 'shortcuts' they could take.

"We already know Mae's *Crabby* isn't the murder weapon. If Bob's is in the china cabinet, that will leave three *Crabby*'s to look for. The *Gull View Inn* will be easy as it's on public display. That leaves Norma and Sally," Dom said.

"I think Sally might have hers at the flower shop. We'll check Norma last." Claire didn't have to say that Norma would probably give them a hard time. Norma could be quite feisty and, even though Claire loved her like family, she didn't look forward to her abrasive response.

"I wonder why Shane said he went straight home?" Claire mused, her finger still scrolling the phone screen. "Bob said Shane headed off to stop Sarah from doing something."

"Bob was drunk. He could have gotten it wrong," Dom suggested. "Or maybe Shane just didn't say anything because he wanted to keep it private."

"Maybe," Claire said. "Anyway, I'm not sure we should spend much time on it. Neither Sarah nor Shane has a motive … and I think I might have found someone who does."

Dom's tingling brows shot up. "Really?"

Claire held the phone up toward him and he glanced over as he pulled into Bob's driveway. On the screen was an article in which he recognized Melvin Blunt's name. "What's that?"

"It's a newspaper article from five years ago. As we suspected, Blunt has pulled his tricks on others before.

From what the article says, he did something to ruin a restaurant so he could by it dirt cheap. The middle-aged couple had built the restaurant from sweat equity and their entire life savings was in it. They were left with nothing. Apparently, the daughter of the owners … a Rita Howell … tried to get revenge."

Dom's eyebrows went into tingle overdrive. He twisted in the seat to look at Claire. "What do you mean by revenge?"

"It says here that she tried to kill him."

"And you think she might be here on the island? Wouldn't she be in jail?"

Claire shook her head. "She wasn't found guilty. The defense claimed that Blunt pulled some shenanigans to make her actions seem more deadly than they really were. She was charged with a lesser crime and only served a few months."

"So, she *could* be here," Dom said. "Maybe this Rita was the person Naughton was talking about when he said he was going to finish what *she* started."

"It's possible. We should look into it."

Dom made a face. "Yeah, but if you were going to an island to kill an old enemy whom you were already accused of attempting to kill, would you use your real name?"

"Good point." Claire held up the phone and pointed to two boxes with x's in them. "These are pictures. Maybe one of them is of Rita. We can take it around to the hotels and businesses and see if anyone recognizes her."

"That sounds like a good plan, but why don't they show up?"

"It's this darn spotty cell phone service. The phone won't stay connected long enough for them to download." Claire put the phone on the dashboard again. "I'll leave it here while we go look for the *Crabby*. Maybe the pictures will be there by the time we come back."

Bob Cleary's house was one of the island's original, old sea captain's homes. He'd inherited it from his grandmother, who'd inherited it from her grandmother. The three-story house was covered with a hundred coats of white paint, the windows flanked by black shutters. The grounds had thick, mature landscaping. Lilac bushes, too late in the season for their scented blooms, reached up to the second floor. The rhododendrons, with their shiny green leaves, grew in a compact row along the front of the house.

As they approached, Dom saw something moving in the back of the house. He peered into the thick growth, his senses on full alert. He could barely make out the shape of a person running toward the woods about a hundred feet from the house. And then it was gone, obscured by the trees. Or maybe it was just his eyes playing tricks on him. "Was that someone running from the house?"

Claire was looking in that direction, too. "I saw the trees moving, but not a person. The walking trails are back there, though. Maybe it was a jogger."

"Probably. Who would be running away from us, anyway?"

Claire laughed. "Right. We aren't with the police anymore. People don't run when they see us like they used to."

They fought their way past the thick shrubs on the side of the house. As they emerged from the bushes, Claire's arm shot out, stopping Dom from walking any further.

"What is it?" he asked.

"Look." Claire pointed to the screen door leading from the back patio into the house. It was ajar, hanging open as if someone had rushed out hastily and forgotten to close it. A breeze kicked up and the door creaked as it swung open further, revealing the six-panel glass door behind it.

Dom felt an electric tingle buzz through him. That door was also ajar—almost closed as if someone had just missed pulling it shut all the way. Dom glanced in the direction he thought he'd seen the person running. It was too late to give chase. The person was long gone by now.

The patio was bare except for two white plastic chairs and a grill. A bachelor's patio with no female touches of nicety. A worn welcome mat sat in front of the door. Dom figured it had been there for years, probably since Bob's wife had lived in the house.

He stepped over to the mat, taking care not to touch or disturb anything. He lifted the corner, nodding to himself in satisfaction when it revealed what he suspected. The concrete under the mat was damp and dark except for one small spot near the corner. That spot was in the shape of a key.

"I think we interrupted someone," Dom said.

"Yes, and look where they were." Claire was standing at the dining room window, her hands cupped over her eyes. The antique oak china cabinet sat against the far wall, its door hanging open. Porcelain shards lay on the floor in front of it—the remnants of at least one piece of Bob's grandmother's antique china.

Apparently, the china cabinet had been the thief's objective. It was crowded with dishes, vases and silver, but right smack in the middle of the top shelf was a big, empty space. Dom guessed most of the items had been passed down through the Cleary generations and were, therefore, valuable antiques.

But, if that was the case, why wasn't more of it missing?

Dom stepped over to another window and looked in the living room. "This room looks fine. Nothing is disturbed."

"Same here in the den." Claire had moved to a room on the other side of the patio.

"We must have interrupted him before he could get to the rest of the house." Dom went back to look in the dining room window. "And he only got as far as this room."

"Yeah, and he didn't even get much. The shelves are still full."

"Yeah, except there is one item missing that we know should be in there."

"The *Crabby*."

Chapter 17

Claire and Dom waited out front for the police to arrive. They'd debated going into the house, but they didn't want to suffer Zambuco's wrath by contaminating the scene. Besides, they'd already gotten the information they'd come for.

"So, either someone stole the *Crabby* or it wasn't there because Bob had already used it as the murder weapon and ditched it." Claire reached through the passenger window of the car and grabbed her phone from the dashboard. A prickle of excitement bloomed in her chest when she saw the very top of the pictures had filled in. It was only one thin line, but at least there was some progress.

"Maybe Bob hired someone to make it look like someone broke in and stole it," Dom mused. "Or maybe someone really did break in and only had time to grab one thing, so they took the biggest object."

Claire snorted. "Good luck to them if they think they're going to be able to turn that into money. It's just base metal."

"Okay, so no one would break in and steal it for money. Why else would they steal it?" Dom asked.

"Good question." Claire jiggled the phone impatiently as if that would speed up the download. "Maybe it wasn't there to begin with."

"Which points toward Bob as the killer."

"Or Shane." A rock lodged in Claire's chest. She was glad the focus was off of Tom and Mae, but she didn't want it to be Bob or Shane. "Bob didn't seem nervous when we asked him about the *Crabby*. If he clonked Blunt with it, I would think there would have been some nervous tick or tell when we asked where his was, and I didn't see one. Not even a flinch."

"Maybe a third party who came to visit Bob earlier in the week took it." Dom nodded toward Claire's phone. "Maybe Bob knows this Rita person and she came to visit."

"Wouldn't Bob notice it was gone?"

Dom pursed his lips. "Not necessarily. You know how it is when you have something that's been in the same spot for years. You kind of forget all about it. Unless he was looking specifically, he might not notice. And that china cabinet is crammed full, so it's easy to glance at it and not think anything is amiss."

"I doubt this Rita person could have put Blunt in

the crab boil pot by herself. She must have had an accomplice."

"Maybe she got Bob to help her. If he really was drunk, his judgment would have been impaired."

"But if he was that drunk, how could he even function enough to be of help?"

"Good point. Maybe she's in cahoots with Naughton," Dom suggested.

"But why would they break into Bob's *now*? They would have broken in *before* Blunt was killed to get the *Crabby* to use as a murder weapon."

"Maybe they did get it before and were breaking in this time to put it back where the police could find it to frame him. We pulled up and they got scared and ran out without being able to replace it."

Claire watched the brown and tan police cruiser pull onto the street. "Maybe. I think we should keep our theories to ourselves, though. Except this newspaper article, if it points to a non-islander, I'm all for the police turning their focus in that direction."

"Agreed."

The police car pulled into the driveway and Zambuco and Robby got out. Zambuco scowled at Dom and Claire. "What's going on? Did you call in a break in?"

"Yes, out back," Dom said.

Zambuco turned his glare on Robby. "Go check it out."

Robby did as told, taking the two uniformed police officers who had arrived in a separate car with him.

Zambuco watched them for a second, then turned

back to pierce Claire with his beady, black eyes. "What were you two doing here?

"We came to visit Bob Cleary."

"And you went to his backyard instead of using the front door?"

"Actually, when we pulled up, we thought we saw someone running off that way." Dom pointed to the woods. "It seemed like he came from the back of the house, so we went out back and found the break-in."

"Do you have any idea who it was?"

"No."

Zambuco folded his arms over his chest and leaned against the hood of his car. "Gee, I'm surprised you two super sleuths didn't give chase."

"He was too far away already," Claire shot back.

"And where is Bob?" Zambuco asked.

"Not home. He must be on his boat. I guess I got the schedules mixed up." Claire plastered a look of wide-eyed innocence on her face.

Zambuco looked at her like he didn't believe her. "Did you go inside?"

"Who, us? No. We know better than that," Dom said.

"This visit wouldn't be related to the Blunt murder, would it?"

Claire fiddled with her phone, her eyes on the display. "No. It was just a social call."

Zambuco pushed off the hood of the car and craned his neck at Claire's phone. "What's that you're doing?"

"I found an article about Blunt. It seems he has a history of playing dirty to get real estate. And one of his victims tried to kill him before."

Zambuco's eyes lit up. "Tell me more."

They stood with their heads bent, watching the pictures fill in at an agonizingly slow pace as Claire summarized the article for him.

"What are you doing?" Robby stood behind Claire. She showed him the phone and brought him up to speed.

He screwed up his face and held out his hand. "Let me see that. My guy didn't find anything about this."

Claire handed over the phone. "Well, I did have to wade through a lot of search results before I found it."

"So you think this Rita person could be on the island and somehow involved in the killing?" Robby used his finger to scroll through the article.

"Yes, we're hoping we can show the picture around to the hotels. It's possible she used a fake name."

"Like Naughton," Robby said.

Claire's brows tugged together. "His name's not Naughton?"

"Nope," Zambuco cut in. "We can't find any Thomas Naughton from Michigan where he claims to be from. He's an impostor, probably using a fake name because he's come to the island for nefarious reasons."

"Like murder?" Dom asked.

"Right, and he might be teamed up with this Rita person." Zambuco was being uncustomarily cooperative with them. Usually, he'd just take their information and tell them not to butt in anymore. Claire wondered if his new semi-nice persona had anything to do with Jane.

"If she was arrested before, she'll be in the database," Zambuco said. "We can go back to the police station and look her up and get her picture that way."

"Good idea." Claire opened the car door.

Zambuco's bushy brows knit together. "Not you. Me and Robby. This is police business and we don't need you to *help*."

"Well, I just thought that being an islander and all, I might be able to recognize her if she's from around here," Claire said.

"No need. *We'll* show the picture around and see if anyone recognizes her." Zambuco started toward his car.

"I don't think we'll need to do that." The tone in Robby's voice stopped Zambuco in his tracks.

Claire looked questioningly at Robby, who held the cell phone up to face them. The pictures had filled and what Claire saw made her stomach plummet.

Rita Howell was Sarah White.

Chapter 18

Zambuco and Robby left the uniformed officers to process the break-in and rushed over to *Chowders*. Dom's heart sank for Sarah as he and Claire followed them. He'd come to think of her as a daughter, probably because his own daughter was about the same age and he didn't see her as often as he liked. Sarah filled that gap for him. Plus she made a mean Italian dessert.

He'd known Sarah was hiding something, but he couldn't believe she was a murderer. Yet, there it was in black and white on the phone. She'd tried to kill Blunt before.

She'd lied about her name and her past. But Dom knew she wasn't violent by nature. If she'd killed Blunt, she must have been pushed to it.

It all made sense now. The twine, the fight with Blunt, the way Shane had had to stop her from doing *something*. Well, it looked like he didn't stop her. Maybe he'd even helped her.

Sarah's face registered alarm when they all walked through the door. Did Dom detect a flicker of guilt?

He stood just inside, trying to read her expression as he inhaled the heavy aroma of mashed potatoes and gravy, the savory smell of the comfort foods a deep contrast to the purpose of their visit. His gaze flicked around the restaurant, which was empty except for one couple at a corner table. Dom felt relieved for Sarah—even if she was a killer, he didn't want to see her humiliated in front of a restaurant full of customers.

"What is it?" Sarah asked. Light glinted off the large knife in her hand which hovered over a pile of half-chopped carrots.

"We need to talk to you about Melvin Blunt," Robby said softly.

Sarah's eyes flicked to Dom and then back to Robby. "I told Dom, don't know anything about him."

Disappointment settled on Dom like a heavy cloak. In his mind, he'd made excuses for her lie about the argument with Blunt, figuring that she might have had a reason to keep it private. Before Blunt was murdered, that didn't seem as important. But now, with the police directly questioning her and knowing who she really was, Dom couldn't help but feel that her lies were a sign of guilt.

Surely, she must know that the police would have figured out who she was, eventually? Then again, if it wasn't for Claire's persistent internet search, maybe they wouldn't have.

Zambuco leaned against the counter. "I think we know that's not true, Sarah … or should I call you Rita."

Sarah's knife clattered to the counter. Her wide eyes darted around the room like a frightened bird.

"We found out about what happened with your parents' restaurant," Claire said gently, earning a warning glare from Zambuco. From his years on the force, Dom knew that investigating officers didn't like others cutting in on their interrogation and Zambuco was no different. And this *was* an interrogation, much as Dom hated to think it.

Dom's stomach twisted as he watched Sarah's face crumble, just before her pale hands flew up to cover it. He instinctively rushed behind the counter to comfort her, just as he would have had he seen his daughter in such distress. On his way, he couldn't help but glance at the shelves under the counter where he'd seen Sarah place the ball of twine. Much to his surprise, the twine was still there.

"That restaurant was my parents' life-long dream," Sarah sobbed.

Dom eased his arm around her shaking shoulders and she sagged against him. "Now, now. We know Blunt didn't play fair. Did he do something to make your parents lose the restaurant?"

Sarah nodded, then reached for a napkin and blew her nose loudly. Her words came out in short bursts between sobs. "My parents ran a clean place. It was their pride and joy. Blunt approached them about selling out. He wanted to build a strip mall or something. They wouldn't sell, but he kept pestering them. He got more and more persistent each time."

"That's too bad," Zambuco said unsympathetically. "I'm more interested in how you tried to kill him, though."

"I didn't! He made up a sto—"

The door flew open and Shane burst in. His face darkened as he looked around at them.

"What's going on here?" he demanded. Then, upon seeing Sarah's tear-stained face, he rushed to her side. Dom gently handed her over and watched as Sarah sunk her head onto Shane's shoulder and produced a new batch of tears.

Shane patted Sarah's blonde hair and glared at them. "Well?"

"It seems you're girlfriend here has another identity," Zambuco said.

Shane didn't even flinch. "That's not true. Not technically."

Zambuco's left brow shot up.

Sarah raised her head from Shane's shoulder, grabbed another napkin and blew into it. "I changed my name legally after what happened with Blunt."

"What, exactly, *did* happen?" Claire asked.

Shane and Sarah exchanged a glance that told Dom either Shane knew everything about Sarah's past, or they'd worked up a story together. He glanced at Claire. She was watching the couple closely, probably thinking the same thing he was. Dom knew she would put her training to good use to detect any tell-tale signs of lying.

"You should tell them everything, right from the beginning," Shane suggested to Sarah.

A Crabby Killer

Sarah gave a shaky nod. "Like I said, my parents' restaurant was their pride and joy. They'd saved their whole lives to open it. When Blunt came around wanting to buy the property, he wouldn't take no for an answer. He became more and more aggressive. Then one day, the health inspector made a surprise visit. Rats were found in the kitchen. We knew there were no rats and we suspected that Blunt had somehow planted them in there.

"The restaurant was closed down until it could be cleaned out and inspected again. But the inspector's schedule was too tight—we think he was paid off or influenced somehow by Blunt to delay it—and the restaurant was closed for months. It was my parents' only source of income and with no money coming in, they defaulted on the mortgage and lost the property. Blunt scooped it up at a discount."

Dom's fists tightened in anger at Blunt.

Claire made sympathetic clucking noises. "And then what happened?"

Sarah sniffed loudly. "Shortly after that, Daddy had a fatal heart attack. I know it was losing the restaurant that did it to him. Mom went into a deep depression." Sarah wrung the napkin in her fist, contorting and twisting it violently. "I hated Blunt for what he'd done to my family."

"So you tried to kill him," Zambuco said.

Sarah shook her head. "No. Well, I admit I did go a little crazy, but I wasn't trying to kill him. I was just trying to make his life as miserable as he'd made mine."

"How?" Claire asked.

Sarah looked down at the floor. "I'm not proud of this, but I resorted to some of the same tricks he'd used.

I had a friend of mine sabotage the concrete of the foundations for his strip mall so that it wouldn't dry properly. I put dead mice in his pool. And I let the air out of his tires."

Zambuco's brows snapped together. "That can't be the full story. We know you tried to kill him."

"I didn't try to kill him." Sarah shot them a pleading look. "You guys know me. You know I'm no murderer."

"But you were arrested. You even went to trial," Zambuco said. "That wouldn't happen if they didn't have concrete evidence."

Sarah sighed. "Blunt orchestrated that, too. When I let the air out of his tires, I didn't let out enough, so he didn't notice they were low and he drove the car. Unfortunately, the tire blew out and he got into an accident. He wasn't killed—he was barely even hurt but someone had seen me let the air out. He suspected I'd been sabotaging his efforts and he used the fact that I'd let the air out of the tires to accuse me of attempted murder. If you read the article you know that the jury did not find me guilty because I wasn't actually trying to kill him, just make him miserable."

"Maybe you weren't trying to kill him *then*." Zambuco stabbed his thick fingers in the air toward her. "But obviously your murderous tendencies escalated. When you saw him on the island here, you saw a second chance to do him in."

Sarah shook her head. "No. I did see him here on the island. He came to the restaurant to taunt me." Sarah slid wet eyes in Dom's direction. "It's true. I was fighting with him that day, but I didn't want to admit it. I didn't want anyone digging into my past. I had no idea he'd end up dead. I'm sorry I lied to you."

Dom's heart melted. Could Sarah's story be true? Judging by what he'd heard, it was entirely possible, especially considering Sarah's gentle nature. But, if she didn't kill Blunt, then who did?

"Then why are you here under an assumed name?" Zambuco asked.

"It's not an assumed name," Sarah said. "I legally changed my name after the trial. Even though I was acquitted, all anyone remembered was that I was accused. I guess in most people's eyes that automatically makes you a killer. I got sick of people recognizing my name. I had no choice but to change it and move away. It was the only way I could get any peace and start over again."

Zambuco snorted. "Well, that's quite a story, Missy. I have to tell you, though, I've arrested killers who had better stories. Your previous altercations with Blunt, the fact that you assimilated yourself here on the island under an assumed identity and then fought with the victim is enough for me to bring you in."

"Wait a minute!" Shane cut in. "She's been living here for several years. How could she possibly have known that Blunt would eventually show up here? You can't seriously think that this was premeditated?"

Zambuco folded his arms across his chest. "Oh, really? Then tell me, where was Sarah that night? And for that matter where were *you*, Shane? I happen to know that you left Bob Cleary's shortly before the time of the murder after conspiring with Sarah on the phone. But when we asked you about it, you said you went straight home. I think that was a lie. It seems to me the two of you may be in on it together. Or maybe you did it on your own as a favor to your girlfriend. I might have to arrest you *both*."

Dom's gut tightened. He remembered Bob had said Shane was going to stop Sarah from doing something. He didn't want to say that out loud, though, just in case Bob hadn't given the details to Zambuco. He was having a hard time believing that Sarah was the killer, especially since the twine was still there and in light of Sarah's sad story. But, then again, Shane *had* lied to them—and apparently to the police—about where he went after he'd dropped off Bob.

"I did lie," Shane admitted. His eyes flicked to Dom and Claire. "And I'm sorry about that. I just didn't think it had any bearing on the case because Sarah didn't kill Blunt and neither did I."

"Then why did you lie?" Claire asked.

Shane sighed. "Sarah has been very upset that Blunt was on the island trying to take the farms from Mae and Tom the same as he took the restaurant from her parents. She knew that he was using tactics that might be illegal and she wanted to expose him for what he was doing. She thought she could help Mae and Tom from suffering the same fate her parents did.

"She called me while I was bringing Bob home. She'd seen Blunt's car in the public parking lot by the pier. She thought there might be some evidence as to his illegal activities in the car and wanted to break in. I begged her not to, though, because I figured if she stole things out of the car it wouldn't be admissible in court. At least that's how it is on TV."

"Break in? That's funny." Zambuco narrowed his eyes at Sarah. "Bob Cleary's house was broken into just today. You wouldn't have had anything to do with that, would you?"

Dom conjured up images of the empty spot in Bob's china cabinet. Did Sarah and Shane break in and steal the *Crabby*? Sarah couldn't have been the person he'd seen—she wouldn't have had time to get back here so quickly, but Shane showed up much later. Then again, *why* would they steal it? Why would anyone? It didn't make any sense.

"Of course not," Sarah said. "I don't even know how to break into a house. Besides, I've been here all day. You can ask Nancy in the kitchen."

Zambuco turned to Shane. "What about you?"

"Why would I break in?" Shane asked.

Zambuco seemed stumped on that one. "Let's get back to the night of the murder. So, you left Bob Cleary's and rushed over to stop Sarah?"

Shane nodded. "That's right. I talked her out of it and she stayed at my place. But neither one of us went to the pier and neither one of us saw Blunt."

Zambuco twisted his face up. "That's great. So you guys are each other's alibi then? And I'm supposed to believe that?"

Dom was vaguely aware of the door opening behind them. His gut churned for Sarah. He hated that potential customers would see her trying to persuade Zambuco of her innocence, especially if she *was* innocent. Dom imagined this scenario must remind her of the first time she was accused of killing Blunt.

Sarah lifted her chin and looked Zambuco in the eye. "It's the truth."

"I think this is the biggest crock of crab dip I've ever heard." Zambuco gestured to Robby. "Cuff them both and put them in the police car."

Robby's eyes ping-ponged uncertainly from Zambuco to Claire. Dom could tell he didn't think Sarah or Shane had done it. But then again, Robby was born on the island and islanders stuck together.

Robby unhooked the cuffs from his belt and slowly started toward Sarah.

"Hold it right there!" a voice said from behind Dom. "You can't arrest her. She didn't do it."

They spun around to see a blond man standing silhouetted in the doorway.

"And just how do you know that Mr. *Naughton*?" Zambuco accentuated the name, leaving no doubt that he knew it was not the man's real name.

"Because I did it. *I* killed Melvin Blunt."

Chapter 19

Sarah gasped. "Ray! No!"

Claire's head swiveled back to Sarah. She knew the mysterious stranger? And apparently well enough to object to his confession. Claire wondered what Shane thought of that, but a quick glance at his face revealed no emotions. Unlike the rest of them, Shane did not seem surprised at this turn of events.

Clearly Shane, Sarah and this Ray person all knew each other. Were they all in on it together? Thoughts of the *Crabby* at the *Gull View Inn* floated to her mind. She wished they'd stopped there first to make sure it was still on the mantle. But then, how did Bob's missing *Crabby* figure in to this?

"Rita, I'm not going to let you go through the same hell you went through before." Ray held his wrists out toward Robby. "You can arrest me instead."

Robby raised a brow at Zambuco, who was frowning at Ray.

"No!" Sarah rushed over to stand between Robby and Ray. "I won't let you do this."

Zambuco crossed his arms over his chest and cocked his head, his eyes studying Sarah. "I would think you'd be happy to get off the hook, but clearly it looks like you three suspects know each other. That's a mighty strange coincidence."

"I don't need to get off the hook, because I didn't kill anyone," Sarah said. "And neither did Ray."

"How can you be so sure?" Zambuco asked. "Did you know he's here using a fake name? That implies deception. But then, again, you would know about that."

Sarah's cheeks flushed and she looked at the floor. "My name is not fake. I told you I changed it legally."

Zambuco waved his arm. "Whatever. Either way, I've got a guy using a fake name who just confessed to a murder standing in front of me. Protocol says I can't leave a killer lose to wreak havoc on the general public, so I think I need to get him down to the station right away." He glanced at Sarah. "Unless you were with him and can give him an alibi. Then again if you were, I'd be inclined to think you were in on it together."

Ray avoided looking at Sarah. "Rita, just let them take me in. It will get them off your back and I'll get what I deserve," Ray pleaded.

Sarah's tortured eyes sought Shane's and he gave an imperceptible nod. She stepped back and Robby cuffed Ray.

Zambuco grabbed Ray's elbow and started toward

the door. Pausing with his hand on the handle, he looked over his shoulder. "And don't you two go anywhere, either. This whole thing smells like rotten crabmeat and I know there's more to it. Especially since you seem to be so close to the killer, here. Rest assured, we'll find out his real identity and motives and if you two are in on it with him, I'll be back to make sure justice is served."

Zambuco pushed on the door and then rammed into it because it opened inward. He cursed, fumbled with the knob, jerked the door open and then propelled Ray through. Claire turned her attention back to Sarah.

"Sarah … or should I call you Rita?" Claire's voice rose with uncertainty.

Sarah answered in a monotone, her eyes glued to the parking lot where they were putting Ray into the police car. "Sarah, please. I changed my name for a reason and I still want to put all that behind me. I'm Sarah White now."

Claire nodded. "Okay, Sarah. I have to ask. Who was that man and *how* do you know he's not the killer? Why would an innocent man confess to murder?"

"That man is no killer," Sarah said. "I know that because he's my twin brother. He came here because he heard Blunt was coming here. He wanted to shield me from him. He came here to protect me and now he's going to jail for me."

Claire's sharp intake of breath gave away her surprise. Sarah had a twin brother? Beside her, Dom smoothed his eyebrows, his face registering the same level of surprise.

"Well, if that's the case, Zambuco won't be able to

find any evidence to make the charge stick, even if Ray did confess," Dom pointed out.

Sarah's pleading eyes flicked between Claire and Dom. "That may be the case, but I don't trust Zambuco. Ray didn't have anything to do with killing Blunt and neither did Shane or I. I'm begging you to find the real killer before Zambuco trumps up some evidence that sends Ray away for life."

***

"Do you really think this Naughton guy is innocent?" Dom asked later after he and Claire had retreated to the scenic overlook to mull over their plan.

"Howell." Claire fiddled with her phone, holding it away from her body and up in the air.

Huh?"

"His last name must be Howell if he's Sarah's brother."

"Oh, right." It was going to take Dom a while to get used to the idea that Sarah's real name was Rita. Then again, did it really matter? She still wanted them to call her Sarah.

Before they'd left the diner, she'd apologized again and assured them that she'd been 'born' as Sarah White into her new life on Mooseamuck Island and she intended to stay. Or maybe that was all a cleverly crafted lie to illicit their sympathy.

"I'm not sure what to think." Claire pulled the phone back to her lap and studied the display. "At least what she says about Ray being her brother is true." Claire tapped her index finger on the phone. "Right here is the whole story. It sounds pretty close to what Sarah told us. And from the tones of their voices and their body language, it did seem like they were telling the truth."

"So, you didn't see any telltale signs that they were covering up?"

Claire shook her head. "No. I know Sarah. She doesn't fit the profile of a killer. Nor does Shane. Though we have seen other people who didn't fit a killer's profile resort to drastic measures for loved ones. But I don't think that's the case here. However, I can't say the same for Ray because I don't know him at all."

"Let's say it wasn't Ray, Sarah or Shane. Then who was it? Could it really have been Tom and Mae working together?" Dom asked.

Claire snorted. "Are you serious? You don't really think it could have been them, do you?"

Dom sighed. "Knowing them, I don't think so. But we have very few clues to go on and the ones that we do have point in their direction. They had motive. They were both there at the scene of the crime. Tom was there in the bar that night."

"Ray was in the bar that night, too, *and* he fought with Blunt," Claire pointed out.

"Now we know what he meant when he said he would 'finish what she started'. The 'she' he was talking about must have been Sarah."

Claire put her phone down and gazed out at the ocean. "That's right. But I do think it's kind of funny he used those words as a threat— *finish what she started*. If Sarah only intended to make Blunt's life miserable, what did he mean by 'finish'? Or was Sarah lying about the lengths she intended to go to and Ray intended to finish it for her once and for all by killing Blunt off?"

"You might be reading too much into that. He might have blurted that out in the heat of the moment and it sounds more sinister than it was, considering how Blunt ended up in the crab pot." Dom's mind drifted to the twine. "Where would Ray get the twine? Or the *Crabby*, for that matter?"

"Can't you get that twine anywhere?" Claire asked. "We could ask Marj at the General Store who ordered twine, but the amount that was around Blunt's neck wasn't significant so I think the killer could have picked up a remnant anywhere. And, of course, it can be purchased off-island so Ray, or anyone, could have bought it anywhere."

"Good point. Without police resources, it will be hard for us to track that down." Dom felt a pinprick of regret that he no longer had police resources. Those resources had helped him solve many cases. But those police resources were just a small part of solving cases. It was his detective skills that really mattered. Without the skills, the resources were worthless.

Dom straightened his back and smiled. He still had those skills and now he would have an opportunity to put those skills to creative uses that might have been frowned upon when he was police consultant.

"If it was Ray, he could have gotten the *Crabby* right from the *Gull View Inn*. He *was* staying there."

Dom's eyebrows tingled. There was something strange about the *Crabby* being the murder weapon.

There were so few of them and somewhere there was one that was missing a piece. "If Ray took it from the *Gull View*, then why would someone break into Bob's and steal his?"

"Maybe that's not why they broke in. Or maybe the *Crabby* was already missing from Bob's. The break-in could just be a coincidence."

"Or maybe Ray had used the *Crabby* from the *Gull View* to kill Blunt, then stole Bob's to replace that one at the *Gull View* and lay the blame on Bob at the same time."

Dom screwed up his face. "That seems like a pretty complicated plan and how would Ray even know Bob had a *Crabby*?"

"If he is the killer, he used a *Crabby* to do it, so somehow he knew about the prestigious award. He might have seen it on the mantle at the *Gull View*. Maybe he even asked about it and found out who else had one. It's clear that Shane knew who Ray really was as well as the whole story about Sarah's background with Blunt. The three of them had probably met and talked before. In fact, Sarah was probably the person that Velma saw Ray meeting with in the rose garden. Maybe Shane told Ray how Bob was drunk that night and Ray cleverly put two and two together and figured he could try to pin it on Bob. Ray might have even seen Bob in the bar. He was there himself."

"Maybe Ray planned it out ahead of time and he was the one sending the drinks to Bob," Dom mused.

"Everything keeps circling back to Bob. He had the

twine, he had the *Crabby* and he had the motive. The only problem is that, by all accounts, he was too drunk to kill Blunt."

"Or that's what he wanted everyone to think," Dom said.

Claire nodded slowly. "I hate to think that Bob would be so devious, but his business was at risk. Or he might have been set up. I think we need to find out more about what Bob really did that night. Who bought him the drinks? And did he really stay home after Shane dropped him off?"

"And who broke into his house and why," Dom said. "I have a gut feeling that might be the key to the whole thing. We know Blunt was hit with a *Crabby* and we know Bob's was missing."

"But was it missing before the break-in or did the thief take it?"

"I think that's what we need to figure out. Once we do, I think we may know who the killer is."

"But how do we figure *that* out?"

"I can think of only one way." Dom smoothed his tingly brow. "Return to the scene of the crime."

Chapter 20

It would have been easier if they could have gotten information from the cops as to what leads they had on the break-in, but Claire didn't dare call Robby. Besides, she knew they had to learn how to investigate without police assistance if they wanted to keep solving crimes, an endeavor which she was surprised to discover she dearly hoped they would continue.

They parked a few streets away from the house, just in case the police happened by. They figured Zambuco would be mad if he caught them there, so they didn't want their car to be seen.

"We may have to get creative," Dom said as he held up the branch of a rhododendron for Claire to pass under. "We don't have the resources of the police now. But we still have our detecting skills."

"We certainly do. What do we need police resources for, anyway?"

"Police resources *would* help us get into the house and be able to look at the crime scene." Dom studied the back door which the police had shut and, presumably, locked.

Claire stood on her tip-toes to reach into a potted plant that hung from the overhang atop the door. "Or we could just use the key." She removed her hand from the pot to show a house key splotched with dirt. "It helps to be an islander and know where other islanders hide things," she explained at Dom's raised brow look.

She hesitated at the door. "I'm sure the police have already dusted for fingerprints, but I still think we should be careful." She bent down and plucked a wide leaf from a hosta plant and put it over the knob while she inserted the key into the lock and turned it.

The door clicked open and they stepped inside. The only evidence that the police had been there were a few smudges of black fingerprint dust on some of the surfaces. Otherwise, the room looked much the same as it had earlier that day before they had called the police.

"I'm not exactly sure what to look for," Claire admitted and Dom felt a rush of pride that she was asking for his advice. Then again, the discovering of physical clues was more his department than hers.

"I don't think we will find any clues as to who the perpetrator is inside the house. If there were any, the police would have found them and taken them as evidence already. But I did want to look at the china cabinet and see if we could determine whether or not it was the

Crabby that was taken this afternoon." Dom stood in front of the cabinet, tilting his head this way and that as he studied the empty space on the top shelf. He moved to the right side, then the left to view the shelf from different angles. Finally, he bent forward at the waist, his hands behind his back and his nose practically touching the cabinet.

While he was doing that, Claire took a silent inventory of the room. She was a good friend of Molly's and had been to the house many times. That's how she knew Molly kept a key in the planter as well as under the mat. She didn't have a photographic memory like Dom, so she didn't know exactly what had been in the china cabinet, but from what she could remember there was nothing else missing from the room.

"I don't think the thief took anything else," Claire said. "Can you tell whether or not he took the *Crabby*?"

Dom's face was awash with disappointment. "Unfortunately, there are no clues as to when the *Crabby* was taken. You can see the spot where it sat." He pointed to a round, clean spot in the middle of the otherwise dusty shelf. "The dust in front of it has been disturbed in such a way that indicates it was removed recently. The problem is there's no way to tell if that was this afternoon, or two days ago when Blunt was killed."

"Even if we could tell if it was removed two days ago, we still couldn't be sure who actually removed it. It could have been Bob, or it could have been Shane when he dropped Bob off that night. Or it could have been someone who came to visit Bob."

"That's the problem. Our best bet is to go outside and

see if we can find a clue from the thief who fled. I think I can find precisely the route he took through the woods."

They locked up, careful not to touch any of the surfaces and made sure they left everything as it was. Claire wiped the key on her pants before returning it to the pot.

"I believe he took off in this direction." Dom pointed to a narrow path which looked like it had been recently trampled.

"It looks like the police have been all over it," Claire said.

"Yes, that's unfortunate. But maybe the police don't have as keen an eye as we do, and maybe they didn't follow the exact route the perpetrator took. I believe when I saw him from the car, he had angled off to the right towards the river. The walking trail goes to the left, so that might be the path the police searched."

They walked slowly through the woods, their heads moving systematically right to left like synchronized metronomes as they searched for clues: a shoe print, a piece of fiber, a dropped cigarette butt, anything that might give them a lead.

After ten minutes, Dom stopped. "I'm not sure which way he went from here. It's too far to see from the road. It would be impossible to tell which direction we should search in."

Claire sighed. "There's only two of us and we have no equipment. We couldn't possibly do a sweep of this entire area."

"I know, but I hate to give up. This is really the only lead we have."

"But we're not even sure the break-in has anything

to do with the murder. Maybe we should follow up with the twine angle," Claire suggested.

Dom's shoulders slumped in disappointment. "I guess you're right. We should go to the …"

His voice trailed off, his brows tugging together as he looked at something on the ground.

"What is it?" Claire asked.

Dom pushed at something hidden halfway under a leaf with his foot. His face brightened. He bent down to pick it up. Pinching it between his thumb and forefinger, he held it out for Claire to see.

Claire didn't know if the police had searched this area, but she could see why they would have missed this clue. It looked just like something you would expect to see in the woods—an acorn, but Claire knew it wasn't just any acorn. It was a caramel root beer acorn. The same candy that was a favorite of Ray 'Naughton' Howell.

***

"So Ray really is the killer." Claire's eyes were fixed on the acorn.

"Why do you say that?" Dom asked.

"That's one of those caramel root beer acorns that he gave to Velma. And he did confess to the murder." Claire's face fell. "I was hoping he did't do it, for Sarah's sake, but he had a motive *and* he threatened the victim. He did have the opportunity and the means and now we've got this clue that places him here at the break-in."

"But Ray isn't the only one of the suspects that eats this kind of candy," Dom said. "Tom Landry was eating one of these in Mae's kitchen the day Zambuco caught him burying the top of the *Crabby* which, by the way, was the murder weapon."

Claire gave a half shrug. "True, but Ray has the more powerful motive of revenge."

"I don't know," Dom said. "It could be argued that Tom's motive was pretty powerful. He wouldn't want his farm taken away and it seems like he was hell-bent on protecting Mae. The two of them might have been in on it together. I noticed that Mae had the brown twine that was used in the murder."

"So did Sarah. She could have given it to Ray."

Dom's eyes snapped over to Claire's in surprise. He hadn't realized that she'd made note of Mae giving the twine to Sarah. He felt a swell of pride. Claire was becoming quite adept at noticing clues under his tutelage. "But Sarah's is still behind the counter at *Chowders*."

"Mae's was cut into pieces too small to fit around Blunt's neck."

Dom nodded. "And none of this rules out Bob, either."

"For all we know, they're all in on it together."

Dom's brows shot up. "Now, wouldn't that be something."

"Indeed. But I hope that's not the case. We have three clues and now we need to narrow them down."

Claire glanced in the direction of the house. "But it still doesn't explain why someone would steal Bob's *Crabby*. What is the motive there?"

"Good question. Unless Bob is the actual killer and the *Crabby* was already gone before the break-in, the only reason I can think for someone else to steal it is that someone wanted to frame Bob. For some reason, they didn't use Bob's *crabby* in the first place, maybe they couldn't get at it or another one was handy or they didn't even think to frame him until later. And then when they realized the police knew a *Crabby* was the murder weapon, they found a perfect opportunity to frame Bob. Everyone knows Bob lives alone and he's out on his boat most of the day. All the killer had to do was steal Bob's *Crabby*, switch the plaques on the base with the real murder weapon and then plant it where the police could find it."

Claire snapped her fingers. "And then they could put the modified *Crabby* back to replace the one that they stole to commit the murder in the first place!"

"Yes, they would have to do that because with only five *Crabby*'s on the island, someone would soon find theirs was missing. The killer was actually quite ingenious to come up with this."

"Yes, he was, but this still doesn't bring us any closer to his identity."

"Well, it would have to be someone that had access to a *Crabby*, brown twine and these acorn candies."

Claire frowned at the candy. "You know, if we were on the police force I'm not sure we would be able to use this candy as a clue. There's nothing that ties this to the break-in. It could have been laying here in the ground for weeks."

Dom turned the caramel acorn around his fingers, a small smile spreading across his lips. Claire *was* getting good at noticing clues, but she had a ways to go before she could interpret all the nuances like he could.

"I don't think so. This candy is in perfect condition. If it had been here for weeks, or even days, an animal would have eaten it or the weather would have deteriorated it and the insects would be chewing on it. This one is perfect, proving that it must have only been here a few hours."

Clear squinted at the candy. "Good point. I guess you're right. Do you think it's okay if we take it? I mean, the police might need it for evidence. We probably shouldn't have touched it."

"You are correct." Dom looked past the candy at her. "Luckily, one of the perks of not working with the police is that we don't have to do things by the book. We can simply put this back and lead the police to it after *we* figure out who the killer is."

Dom looked at the candy, a satisfied warmth blooming in his chest. He knew this was a good clue, and he knew that he and Claire could ferret out the identity of the real killer. Just like in the old days. "I think we need to find out who else on the island had a fancy for these candies. There can't be too many people who have a taste for the combination of caramel and root beer."

Claire snorted. "You can say that again. It sounds gross."

"Velma said that Ray got these candies from the *Harbor Fudge Shop*. I do believe paying them a visit might be quite informative."

Claire's mouth watered with visions of the *Harbor Fudge Shop*'s famous dark chocolate. She'd eaten the stash Jane had bought her already. She started toward the car. "Well, then, what are we waiting for?"

Chapter 21

It was the last day of the Crab Festival and everyone knew that most of the vendors would have big sales, so the pier was packed to the gills.

Dom and Claire elbowed their way through the crowd. The clamor of conversation, the squeal of children and the smell of popcorn and fried dough filled the air, setting a festive mood. But Claire didn't feel festive. She was on the hunt to find a killer who quite possibly could be one of her longtime friends.

Claire saw Marj Hancock from the General Store duck into a booth. She grabbed Dom's arm. "Marj just went into that tent. Let's go talk to her about the twine."

Dom's brows tugged together. "You don't think she'll remember who bought twine, do you? I mean, she must sell hundreds of items in the store."

"Oh, yes, she will. She has a mind like a steel trap."

Claire picked up the pace, propelling him along, her eyes glued to the spot where Marj had disappeared from view. They passed the *Harbor Fudge Shop* tent, but Claire didn't stop. She didn't want Marj to get away, and they could come back to the *Fudge shop* later.

When they got closer, she realized Marj had gone into Sally Kimmel's florist tent.

Claire turned into Sally's and was immediately enveloped by the perfume of flowers. The multi-tiered displays overflowing with every type and color of flower imaginable made the tent look like a garden oasis. Sticking out from behind a large pot of a tall, spiked cactus Claire recognized the furry striped tail of Porch Cat flicking lazily. Claire envied the cat, who she figured was spending a leisurely day napping among the jungle-like display, but she didn't have time to stop even for a quick scratch behind the ears.

She pulled Dom around a three-tiered stand that boasted white daisies, pink carnations and yellow black-eyed Susans.

Once they cleared the display, Claire pulled up short. In between a giant fern and a topiary, Marj was being accosted by ninety-two-year-old Esther Baines, who made Norma look like an amateur in the crotchety old lady department.

Esther was waving her finger in Marj's face, causing Marj to lean backward precariously. "Now I know I counted out seventy-three pennies at the register and your girl short-changed me."

"I'm sorry, Esther. I'll look into it. I'm sure it was an honest mistake." Marj gave Claire a knowing look.

"I'm out twenty-seven cents!"

Marj dug in the pocket of her jeans. She pulled out a quarter and a nickel. "Here, take these. Keep the change for your inconvenience."

Ester scowled at the money for a minute before plucking it out of Marj's hand. "That sets it right, but 'taint right for your girl to try to swindle an old lady."

Marj did her best to paste a contrite look on her face. "I'm sorry, Esther. You can be sure I'll give her a talking to."

Esther pursed her lips, turned around and started inspecting a display of white roses, lily of the valley and peonies without another word.

Marj rolled her eyes at Claire and shook her head, then the two of them chuckled.

"Esther never changes, does she?" Claire whispered.

Esther whipped her head around. "I heard that."

"Mew!" Porch Cat, apparently disturbed by the argument, thrust out his front legs in a languid stretch. He looked at Marj, Claire and Dom disapprovingly, flicked his tail at Esther and trotted off toward the front of the tent, presumably to find a more suitable place to nap.

Claire watched him trot off, then turned to Marj. "Marj, we have a question."

"Oh?" Marj looked from Dom to Claire. She leaned in and whispered, "Is this about the murder?"

"Well, it might be something that could help." Claire tried to downplay the importance. She didn't want Marj making any assumptions about the twine.

"We were just wondering if you remembered who bought twine recently," Dom said.

Marj's brows rose. Claire didn't know if the police had released the fact that Blunt had been strangled with the twine, but anyone who was on the pier that morning would have seen it and word had probably gotten around.

"The only two that have ordered twine recently are Bob and Donovan. For their boat lines."

Claire didn't know what she'd been expecting for an answer, but this one wasn't very enlightening.

"Did they both buy the brown twine?" Dom persisted.

"No. Just Bob buys brown now. Donovan's been getting the blue ever since he changed his colors at the beginning of the season."

Squeak. Squeak-ity. Squeak.

Sally's son, Jonathan, rode into the tent, miraculously avoiding ramming into the plants as he skidded to a stop in front of them.

"I see your chain is squeaking again." Dom tilted his head to look down at the side of the bike.

"People should really make sure their kids' bikes don't cause such a disturbing racket," Esther said loudly. And just in case her first comment wasn't loud enough for everyone in the tent to hear, she raised her voice another octave and added, "And they shouldn't let their kids out riding them at all hours of the night, either."

Sally came rushing around the corner. She glared at Esther, then addressed Jonathan. "I thought I told you not to ride your bike in here."

Jonathan's face crumbled into a guilty mask and he hopped off the bike. "Sorry, Mom. I forgot."

A Crabby Killer

But Sally had already turned to Esther. "And I don't let Jonathan ride his bike at all hours of the night."

"Are you calling me a liar?" Esther asked.

"No," Sally said. "But I don't like how you insinuated that I don't watch my son. Jonathan puts his bike away every night after supper and he's in bed by nine."

"Harrumph. I happen to know he was out two nights ago in the wee hours of the morning."

Sally scowled at Esther. "What in the world are you talking about?"

"I know what I heard and it was that bike. It was the night before the Crab Fest opened. I had eaten some crab legs with a little too much butter and it didn't sit well. I woke up at two a.m. with heartburn and when I was drinking down my Maalox, I heard that bike's noxious squeaking sound going right by my house over there." Esther pointed in the direction of her house which was the same street as the pier, just a block away.

"You must be hearing things." Sally put a protective hand on Jonathan's shoulder. "I certainly don't let Johnny wander around at two in the morning."

Claire shifted her weight from one foot to the other. Listening to the argument made her uncomfortable. Beside her, she could see Dom nervously smoothing his eyebrows. He must have been uncomfortable, too.

Claire's attention drifted to a high shelf which held dozens of awards. Plaques and trophies were lined up and right smack in the middle sat Porch Cat, slowly licking his paw and rubbing it behind his ear, his eyes narrowed into small slits. Claire felt glad that he'd found a spot where he had a bird's-eye-view of the area and no one would bother him.

Claire's attention returned to the group of people in front of her in time to see Esther stomp off.

"I'm sorry you guys had to see that." Sally, who was obviously flustered, waved a piece of paper in her hand. "I'm a little peeved today. A credit card payment for peat moss got declined and when I looked up my account online, some strange charges appeared. My card is on hold and I can't buy things I need for the shop."

The flap lifted on the back of the tent and Donovan backed in, a small, white bag in his hand. A surprised look crossed his face when he turned to see them all standing there.

"Oh, hi. What are you guys doing?" Donovan's brows dipped as he looked at Jonathan's bike and then from one person to another.

"Just keeping the economy going by coming down to spend our money," Dom said.

"Uncle Donny, Ester yelled at Mommy," Jonathan cut in.

Donavan's lips quirked in a smile and he ruffled Jonathan's hair, then looked up at Sally. "Really? What about?"

The smile quickly disappeared from his face as Sally thrust the piece of paper out toward him. "Who cares about Esther. I want to know about this bill. You need to take it to *Duffy's* and get these charges straightened out because they must be a mistake."

Donovan's face turned red. His eyes darted around the tent. The look on his face told Claire he'd rather be anywhere else but here.

Sally kept after him. "Unless you bought a couple of rounds for the house? You did, didn't you? I knew I shouldn't have let you use my credit card."

Claire felt even more uncomfortable than she had when Esther and Sally were arguing. She wanted to leave, but she couldn't ignore the niggle that was starting right under her ribs. Something was odd about the way Donovan was reacting to the bill.

Dom spoke up. "I remember you did say you drank a lot the night before the Crab Fest opening."

Sally looked down at the paper. "That's when these charges are from. But there must be a mistake. It says you bought nineteen drinks! No one person can drink that many drinks!"

Donovan switched the white bag into his left hand and slowly reached his right out toward the paper. "I'll see what I can do."

Sally reached under a white, cloth-covered table and dragged out a navy blue duffel bag. She struggled with its weight as she shoved it toward Donovan. "And take this bag, someone already tripped over it. What do you have in here anyway? It weighs a ton."

Claire's eyes flicked up to the spot where Porch Cat was still sitting in between all of Sally's awards. The cat looked right at her and Claire could have sworn he winked. Then her eyes flicked to the bike that Jonathan was standing beside.

Dom must have been following the same line of thinking because he pointed to Porch Cat and asked, "What usually goes in that spot where the cat is sitting?"

Sally turned, a look of disgust spreading across her

fine features. "That's where my *Crabby* goes. It turned up missing the first day of the Fest. Can you believe that? Someone came into the tent and stole my award." She flapped her hands against her sides. "Who would do that?"

Everything clicked into place. Claire locked eyes with Donovan. His white candy bag gaped open ... inside nestled a group of caramel root beer acorns.

Things must have clicked for Dom, too. Claire saw him lunge toward Donovan, but the younger man had seen it coming. He threw the heavy duffel bag at Dom, who managed to catch it with a loud grunt as Donovan ran out of the tent.

"What the heck?" Sally's brows mashed together as she stared after Donovan.

Dom dropped the duffel bag and it landed with a thud, then he grabbed Jonathan's bike. "Check the duffel bag. I think you'll find a *Crabby* in there!"

Dom flung his leg over the side of the bike with a burst of agility that belied his age and started off after Donovan amidst the protests of both Claire and Sally. "We can't let him get away—he's the killer!"

Chapter 22

Dom's heart pounded against his rib cage as his thighs pumped the pedals faster and faster. Up ahead, Donovan was running toward the end of the dock where Dom could see he had one of his small Boston Whaler's at the ready.

Had he been planning to make his get-away even before Claire and Dom figured out the truth?

Donovan glanced back, caught sight of Dom on the bike and picked up speed, heading straight for the Whaler. Dom could see the boat was only secured with one rope. Donovan could quickly slip the rope off the cleat, hop on the boat and escape.

Dom willed his thigh muscles to work faster and the bike's squeaks raised in tempo, the tires thap-thaping on the boards of the dock. His fingers, wrapped tightly around the handles bars, tingled from the vibration of the bumpy ride. His legs burned—he hadn't used those muscles in years and he was going to be sore tomorrow, but that didn't matter now. He *had* catch up before Donovan got to the boat.

But what would he do when he reached him? How would he stop the killer? There was only one way. Dom stood on the pedals and gave it his all.

His efforts paid off. He was gaining speed, the gap between him and Donovan rapidly closing.

And then, in one final burst of effort, he aimed right for Donovan. The bike smashed into him at full speed, sending both Donovan, Dom and the bike plunging into the ocean.

The instant chill of the water took Dom's breath away. He'd lost his grip on the handlebars during the collision, which was probably just as well. The bike raced twenty-five feet to the bottom and Dom kicked to the top, his head breaking the water just as Donovan's did the same.

Donovan splashed water into Dom's face, turned and started swimming toward his boat.

"Stop right there!" Dom yelled even as he started after the other man. Of course, Donovan didn't stop, but he was a weak swimmer and Dom caught him easily, grabbing on to the back of Donovan's shirt and trying to haul him back to the dock.

"Let me go, old man!" Donovan writhed and twisted.

"Old man? I'll show you who's old!" Dom tried to grab him in a headlock.

Donovan twisted away, pushing down on Dom's shoulders.

Dom went under, swallowed a mouthful of water and came up coughing. His lungs burned. Through watery eyes, he saw Donovan trying to swim away again but he'd be damned if he'd let some young whippersnapper call him an old man!

Dom pushed after Donovan, grabbing him by the ankle and pulled him back through the water, face down.

Donovan choked and sputtered. He kicked out weakly at Dom and then was still. A jolt of panic shot through Dom. Had he killed Donovan? He let go of the ankle and turned the man over.

Donovan sprang into action as soon as Dom turned him over. It was just a ruse! The younger man punched out, connecting with Dom's face. If they were on dry land, the punch might have hurt more, but the water lessened the force and Dom barely felt a thing. He punched back.

The two men grappled for power in the water. Dom landed a few good blows and managed to dunk Donovan under. Donovan kicked out underwater, grinding a foot in Dom's belly which knocked some steam out of him.

Dom was getting winded, but he could see that Donovan was, too. Now if the police would just come, Dom could probably get Donovan to the dock and hand him over. At the very least, they would block his access to the boat and Donovan would have no choice but to give up.

Footsteps pounding on the dock caught Dom's attention and he made the mistake of turning to look. Donovan seized the opportunity to push him under and this time, he did not let go of Dom's shoulders. The man intended to hold him under water and kill him!

Dom fought the panic that rose in his chest. Remembering a self-defense move he'd learned when he was with the police, he shot his arms up and out, breaking Donovan's hold on his shoulder. His head shot up out of the water and he gulped fresh air.

Why weren't the police, or whoever it was running down the dock, doing something to capture Donovan?

Dom didn't have time to turn around and see what was going on at the dock because Donovan was coming for him again. Dom gulped in a deep breath of air before the other man pushed him under. He lashed out underwater, kicking at Donovan's legs.

Donovan released his grip and Dom shot up again. He managed to land a blow on Donovan's neck that startled the younger man and caused him to pause. Dom took advantage by pushing Donovan's head under, but he could only hold him for a second before it popped up again.

All this fighting and being pushed under the water was tiring Dom out. His movements were getting slower. Weakness washed over him. His muscles were giving out. Over the splashing of the water and the rush of his own blood in his ears, Dom could hear the police sirens. It wouldn't be long now, if only he could hold Donovan back a little longer.

Donovan's face was red with anger—the kind of anger that gives you superhuman strength. He knew he only had a few precious seconds to finish Dom off and get away. Donovan leveraged his feet against a pylon and pushed with all his might knocking his head into Dom's with incredible force.

A Crabby Killer

The blow made Dom dizzy. He tried to tread water, but his arms and legs weren't responding to the signals his brain was sending. Somehow, his fist still managed to clutch part of Donovan's shirt, holding him there for capture.

He turned and glanced over at the pier, relief flooding over him as he saw the blue flashing lights. They were coming ... all he had to do was hold on for a few seconds more.

But it was too late. Like an animal sensing the weakening of his prey, Donovan moved in for the kill and pushed Dom under for the last time.

***

Claire ran down the dock, frantically searching for some kind of weapon she could use to break up the fight between Dom and Donovan, who thrashed in the water beside the dock.

She could see Dom was holding his own, but Donovan was much younger—how long could Dom hold out?

The turbulent sound of splashing water heightened her anxiety as she cast a panicked glance into one of the boats, looking for something she could use to help Dom.

Where were the police? She'd placed the call after Dom had taken off on the bike. As usual, she'd had to hunt for a spot with enough bars for her phone to connect and make the call. That had impacted her ability to rush to Dom's aid. She hoped she'd done the right thing. Dom was her partner and she would never forgive herself if something happened to him, but Sally had been too upset to make a call and Claire knew they needed the police right away, so she'd taken the time to do it herself.

She glanced at the two figures in the water, her heart squeezing as she saw Dom go under. She held her breath until he popped up again. Her eyes fell on a large-handled net in one of the boats. She lunged for it, grabbed the aluminum end in her right hand and ran to the side of the dock.

The police sirens and tires squealing at the end of the dock barely registered as she watched Dom go under again. This time he didn't pop back up.

"Dom!" she yelled. But then, Donovan was swimming toward his boat which Claire had already noticed was set up for a quick get-away.

She planted her toes on the edge of the dock, leaned forward as far as she could and grabbed the pylon with her left hand to keep from falling in the water. With her right hand, she slapped the net over Donovan's head, her eyes frantically scanning the water for Dom.

Donovan's hands flailed at the net. "Hey, let me out!"

Claire stood her ground. Donovan's struggle nearly pulled her into the water, but she couldn't let him get away. Thankfully, he was tangled up in the net, unable to simply duck underwater to escape. He struggled to swim forward, though, but the resistance of the water made his movements ineffectual against the force of the net.

"Auntie Claire!" Robby was at her side and grabbing the net from her hands. She'd been using the pylon to balance the forward pressure of Donovan pulling on the net and when Robby took it, Claire fell backwards, landing her butt on the hard wooden dock with a thud

"Ooomph!"

"Sorry. Are you okay?" Robby turned concerned eyes on her.

"Never mind about me," Claire said as Zambuco joined them. "He pushed Dom under and he hasn't come back up!"

"Where?" Zambuco asked, a surprising amount of concern in his dark eyes.

"Right about here." Claire pointed to the spot she'd seen Dom go under. She peered over the side of the dock into the water looking for him. But the water was murky, all stirred up from the altercation.

Was Dom down there somewhere? Should she jump in?

"Over there!" Zambuco pointed a stubby finger to the other side of the dock where Dom bobbed in the water. Dom shook his head. Droplets of water flew off his gray hair. He made a wheezing choking sound and coughed up some water.

Relief washed over Claire. She rushed to the other side of the dock and knelt down, extending her hand. "Grab my hand. I'll help you get up on the dock."

Dom paddled closer. "What happened to Donovan?"

Claire glanced behind her. "Zambuco and Robby have him on the other side of the dock. We got him."

Dom reached out for her hand, then bracing himself against the pylon, he let her help him up onto the dock where he collapsed. Behind them, Zambuco and Robby had wrestled Donovan onto the dock where he lay facedown with his hands behind his back.

Donovan glared over at Claire and Dom. "If it wasn't

for you old farts meddling, I would've gotten away."

"Old farts?" Claire frowned at Donovan. "I guess us old farts got the best of you, didn't we. And I hope they throw the book at you."

Donovan scoffed. "No. I don't think the way you captured me was legal. I'll sue. I'll fight this. I'll have *you* put in jail."

"Now, now, don't be so *crabby*." Zambuco jerked the cuffs and Donovan winced. "Dom and Claire did us a big favor."

Claire looked at Zambuco incredulously. Did he just admit that she and Dom had helped him out?

Dom's eyes fell on the net now laying on the dock in a pool of water. "How exactly *did* you capture him, anyway?"

Claire laughed. "When I got here, I saw the two of you fighting. I grabbed the first thing I thought could help which happened to be this net. He had pushed you under the water and I did the only thing I could think of. I slipped the net over his head. You must have tired him out and he got trapped in the net and couldn't maneuver out of it, so I held him there until Robby came and fished him out."

"You caught the killer with a net?"

Claire laughed. "I guess it seems appropriate, eh?" She turned concerned eyes on Dom. "What happened to you? How did you end up on the other side of the dock?"

Dom's brows tugged together. "I'm not sure. I remember I was feeling very weak from fighting. He kept dunking me under and that one last time, I must have passed out for a while. I guess I must have floated under the dock. Then I came to on the other side." Dom shrugged. "I'm bummed out that I missed the capture."

"You did the important part," Claire assured him. "You stopped him from getting on the boat and held him at bay. I just finished the job. It was teamwork."

"And a fine piece of teamwork it was, too. The whole investigation was, actually." Dom smiled proudly, then held out his knuckles.

Claire met them with her own. "I concur."

Behind them, Robby and Zambuco were pulling Donovan, who was still mumbling about how he was going to 'get back at' Claire and Dom, to his feet.

Robby said, "We're going to take him in. Are you two okay?"

Dom and Claire looked at each other. They'd caught another killer and that was more than okay with Claire. She figured it was more than okay with Dom, too. They both nodded at Robby.

"All right, then," Zambuco said. "We'll take this one off to jail where he belongs, but don't either of you leave the island. I'll need statements."

Donovan issued another string of complaints and Robby jerked him along. "Stop being so grumpy. They caught you fair and square."

"That's right." Dom glared at Donovan. "We know you killed Blunt and I think once the police look inside your duffel bag, they'll know that you're also the one who broke into Bob Cleary's house to steal his *Crabby*."

They watched Zambuco and Robby lead the struggling Donovan down the length of the dock. Even from behind, they could see Donovan was mouthing off the whole way.

"I don't think prosecuting Donovan is going to be an easy task despite all the evidence against him," Claire said.

"Nope, he's going to fight it as much as he can."

Claire stood, brushed off her jeans and offered her hand to Dom to help him up. "I bet he makes them miserable down at the police station. You know, the type that complains about everything and makes a lot of demands."

"Oh, yes, I know the type." Dom watched a stream of water pour out onto the dock as he wrung out the bottom of his shirt. "We've seen plenty of those, but with Donovan we don't have to listen to it."

"That's right," Claire said brightly. "He's Robby and Zambuco's problem now. One big benefit to not being officially on the case is that we don't have to deal with the paperwork or any of the technicalities. We just get to do the fun part—catch the killer."

"That's a definite bonus," Dom agreed. "And we don't have to deal with the killers pleading, whining and lying after they're arrested, which in this case is a very good thing because it looks like we netted ourselves one crabby killer."

Chapter 23

Zambuco held the chestnut-colored candy up to the light, his thick thumb and forefinger practically obscuring the entire piece. "So, the killer was tripped up by a candy," he said in wonder.

"We should have figured it out before. The clues were all there," Claire replied.

"Caught with a net from his own boat." Tom Landry, seated across the long, wooden table from Claire shook his head. Claire couldn't help but smile when she noticed he and Mae were seated next to each other, their chairs awfully close.

Her smile turned into a frown when she noticed Jane sitting awfully close to Zambuco. She made a mental note to talk to Jane about what was going on with the ornery detective, as well as her recent extravagance with money. A pang of guilt shot through her—had she been so involved investigating cases that she had ignored what was going on with her best friend?

A light breeze swept up from the ocean. The briny scent, mingled with that of seafood, garlic and spices, ruffled Claire's hair, making the humid summer night bearable. There was something to be said for air conditioning, but Claire still preferred to dine outside, as they were doing now in a private preview of *Chowders* new outdoor dining patio.

Sarah had prepared a special feast to celebrate the patio's first use as well as her brother being freed from jail. Claire watched as Sarah balanced plates of food on her way to the table, her smile wider than Claire had ever seen it, her stance much more relaxed.

This whole thing with Blunt had turned out to be a blessing in disguise for Sarah. She'd told Claire that she had hated having to lie to them to keep her past a secret. Now that everything was out in the open, and the islanders thought no less of her for her past actions, she felt a huge sense of relief. Now she could really settle in, make the island her home and focus on making improvements to *Chowders*, something she didn't want to invest in before, in case she had to cut and run.

Not only that, but her brother Ray looked like he was going to be staying on Mooseamuck Island, too, and that made Sarah even happier.

"Woof!"

The golden retriever puppy Claire had seen in the animal rescue tent sat at the edge of the patio, his tail thumping wildly on the grass. Claire knew Sarah had bonded with the dog when she'd seen them that day at the Crab Fest. Sarah had used the restaurant as an excuse, but later on confessed that the real reason she didn't adopt him was because she was always afraid that she might have to leave town quickly. She didn't think it was fair to adopt the dog when circumstances might force her to give him up. But now, with that threat gone, she knew she could give the dog a loving and healthy forever home.

Claire's heart warmed as she watched Sarah bounce over to the dog, who she had named Providence, and scratch him behind the ears. The dog looked up at Sarah adoringly and Claire saw that adoration mirrored in Sarah's eyes as she slipped him a steak tip.

Claire dipped her spoon into the steaming clam chowder and sipped in a small amount. It was salty, creamy and the chunk of clam made for a chewy, satisfying taste.

"It's terrible what Donovan did," Mae said. "I hate to think that one of our own islanders killed someone so brutally." She looked sideways out of the corner of her eye and added, "Even if he did deserve it."

"It's not so much that," Jane added. "But he tried to frame Bob Cleary. Killing someone as mean and nasty as Blunt … well, that's one thing, but an islander framing another islander—there's just no excuse for that."

"And poor Sally." Alice held her knitting in her left hand while she balanced a crab cake in her right. "She must feel awfully betrayed by her brother."

"Yes, it was cowardly for him to use her as an alibi and steal his nephew's bike to commit the crime," Norma said. "I can't abide by something like that, even though

Sally will come out okay in the end. I hear she's taking over *Crabby* Boat Tours and she'll have that place shipshape in no time. Donovan wasn't very good at running the family business. It was going downhill, but under Sally's expert guidance, I think they'll do quite well."

Jane nodded. "I agree. Who'd a thunk Donovan would stoop so low."

"What I don't get," Norma said as she dipped a steamed clam in broth, then butter and dropped it into her mouth, "is how he could have had it planned all along. I mean, how would he have known that Blunt would have been in the bar that night so he could kill him and put him in the crab boil pot?"

Zambuco snuck a fried clam from Jane's plate. "That part was just a matter of good timing. He had known he was going to kill Blunt for months. In fact, that's why he redid his whole boat line in the blue colors. Donovan used to use the brown twine, but he had to change colors to point suspicion at Bob. He was planning on framing Bob all along, because he knew Bob would have the same motive. And with Bob out of the way, Barnacle Bob's tours might go under, which would give him a monopoly on the boat tour business.

"Donovan knew that Blunt was planning on opening the tour boat business and, since his was doing badly, he knew it would put him under. He also knew Blunt would eventually come to the island. He didn't know exactly when, but he'd set the wheels in motion ahead of time so he would be prepared when the time came."

"That's right," Dom added. "He just got lucky with

the Crab Fest. When he saw both Blunt and Bob in the bar that night, he knew he had the perfect opportunity."

"But he had to get Bob out of the way, and create an alibi for himself," Robby chimed in. "So, he pretended to be drunk. He actually poured his drinks into the plant on the windowsill, which is now quite dead."

"And he sent drinks anonymously to Bob, but he got them delivered to his table first and spiked them with rohypnol, then had the waitress take them over. He needed to put the drug in because he needed Bob to not be able to remember what he did that night."

"So Donovan pretended that he was too drunk to drive and he stayed over at Sally's?" Alice asked.

"That's correct. Once Sally and Jonathan were asleep, he took the bike and rode back to *Duffy's*. Lucky for him, Blunt was still inside. We're not exactly sure of the chain of events because he refuses to say much, but he grabbed Sally's *Crabby* out of her tent, got the twine that he'd been saving up and then waited for the bar to close so he could confront Blunt.

"According to what little he told us, he kept Blunt talking for quite some time. He pretended like he was going to sell him his own boat business on the cheap. He had seen the crab pot earlier in the day and figured that would be a great place to hide the body and, hopefully, add confusion to the investigation. Once he got down there, he knocked Blunt out with the *Crabby*, lifted him into the pot and then strangled him to finish him off," Zambuco said.

"We don't know if he planned to use the *Crabby* all

along or the idea came to him that night, but either way it was premeditated murder," Robby added.

"I didn't realize he was so devious. But what's the significance of the candy?" Norma nodded to the caramel root beer acorn, now laying on the napkin beside Zambuco's plate.

"A candy like this tied him to the break-in at Bob Cleary's and proves his intention with the *Crabby*." Zambuco picked it up and then narrowed his eyes at Dom and Claire. "What I don't get is how you knew Donovan had left one of these candies behind at Bob Cleary's. There was no reason for the two of you to go back there … unless you were investigating."

Zambuco popped the candy into his mouth while Claire struggled to come up with a valid reason for why they went back to Bob's. She'd thought they'd gotten off the hook on that one. After Donovan had been captured on the dock, Claire and Dom had gone home and changed out of their wet clothes, then gone together to the police station and given their statements.

The police had found the *Crabby* in the duffel bag and Dom had told them his and Claire's suspicions had been confirmed when they'd seen Donovan eating the very candy they'd found on the path outside of Bob's. Zambuco hadn't asked what made them go back there at the time and they'd thought they had gotten off scot-free.

Claire glanced at Dom for help, but they were saved from answering when Zambuco screwed his face up into a tormented grimace.

"Blech. This thing tastes awful." He spit the candy out into a napkin. "Who eats these things? No wonder

Donovan was driven to kill someone."

Claire said, "That's how we knew that candy was from him. Not too many people eat them, as you can see. And the reason we were there is—"

Zambuco held up his hand. "Save it. I don't even want to know. The truth is that the two of you did help us out quite a bit and I have to admit I'm grateful for it. Maybe we could even utilize your consulting services sometimes ... I could use some extra hands, especially with the alarming rate people get murdered on this island."

Claire and Dom exchanged raised-brow looks. Was Zambuco serious? She couldn't believe he was actually giving them accolades in front of everyone. Beside him, she noticed Jane beaming proudly. Was she responsible for Zambuco's change in behavior?

"Thanks," Claire said uncertainly. "I have to say we could have put it together sooner, but I never imagined that Donovan would fake his alibi and use Jonathan's bike to do it. You see, I noticed he had grease on his pants leg when we talked to him the day after the murder, but I didn't put two and two together at the time. I thought the grease smear was from something on the boat, but it was from Jonathan's faulty bicycle chain."

Dom frowned. He had noticed the greasy pant leg, too, and had also not put two and two together. He could forgive it in Claire because that was not her department but *he* was supposed to be the one who noticed the clues. He made a mental note to be more observant next time.

"We really had no reason for that to make us suspicious at the time. It wasn't until later on when Esther mentioned she'd heard Jonathan's bike squeaking in the middle of the night that we realized Donovan had used it to get back to the pier," Dom said.

Norma dropped another clam into her mouth. "That really gets my ire up that he used the little boy's bike. I hear it's at the bottom of the cove now."

"Dom used it to catch Donovan and knock him in the water," Mae smiled at Dom. "And he was nice enough to buy him a brand new one to replace it. He's a real hero in my book."

Dom blushed. "Well, I don't know about that. There was another clue that we missed. Might have caught him sooner and been able to avoid chasing him into the water had I paid more attention."

"What was that?" Norma asked.

"Claire had seen Donovan fighting with Blunt on the docks the day before Blunt was killed. When we asked him about it, he said they were fighting about the baseball game. Donovan, like everyone else on the island, is a huge Red Sox fan and he said that Blunt was a huge Yankees fan and they'd fought about which team was best. But when we talked to Floyd in the bar, he said Blunt was *jeering* the Yankees. He wasn't a Yankees fan at all. Donovan lied about the subject of their argument because they were really arguing about Blunt's intention to launch a tour boat business. Naturally, Donovan didn't want to let on that he knew about that as it would give him a motive. Unfortunately, I didn't pick up on that at the time."

Claire frowned. *She* hadn't picked up on him lying, either. She could forgive it in Dom because that was not his department. She was the one who was supposed to notice when people were lying. She made a mental note to be more observant next time.

"What's all this business with the *Crabby*, though?" Norma asked. "Tom buried the top of it to protect Mae, but the murder weapon wasn't even her *Crabby*. Then Donovan stole Sally's and Bob's. What's up with that?"

"Tom found the top of the *Crabby* next to the crab boil pot when the committee met there that morning," Claire said. "He knew Blunt had been threatening Mae's farm and when we saw Blunt's body in the pot, he panicked, thinking it might incriminate Mae."

"And he picked up the evidence to save me." Mae beamed at Tom who blushed and ducked his head.

"But it turned out it wasn't Mae's *Crabby* that did the killing," Zambuco said. "Hers was in the basement and still intact."

"Donovan had used Sally's but I think he planned to make the switch and frame Bob all along," Dom said. "He'd already orchestrated things so that Bob had no alibi. And Bob had a motive *and* he used the brown twine. Donovan knew Sally had her *Crabby* in the tent at the Crab Fest and it was easy to get to. He used that one to clonk Blunt on the head, but he didn't want to incriminate Sally, so he stole Bob's *Crabby*, intending to switch the tops, then return Sally's and plant Bob's—now with the broken, incriminating, top—on one of his boats where it could later be found by the police."

Jane shook her head. "Poor Bob."

"And Sally," Mac added.

"Oh, I think they might make out okay." Norma nodded toward the street where Bob and Sally were walking, ice creams in hand and heads bent together.

"Maybe Bob and Sally are getting together to join forces in the boat tour business," Jane mused. "Donovan had a big ego and always tried to compete with Bob, but I know Bob always thought they could do better if they worked together instead of against each other."

Norma craned her neck to watch the couple as they walked out of view. "That may be, but I suspect they may be thinking about combining more than just the businesses."

"Well, that will end a decades-long feud and probably be good for both of them." Alice finished off the row she was working and stuffed her knitting project into her large tote bag.

"I guess Blunt's death might have actually done some good." Tom put his hand over Mae's. "It seems to have caused more than one feud to be ended."

"And it helped Sarah get her life back," Jane nodded toward Sarah who was approaching with a loaded dessert tray.

"Anyone for dessert?" Sarah winked at Dom. "I have some special Italian pastries for you to try."

***

Everyone enjoyed a healthy helping of dessert and then started to take their leave. Mae and Tom had driven down from their farms together, so they left at the same time, and Zambuco made up some lame excuse to leave right after Jane. The rest of them drifted off one by one until it was only Dom and Claire left at the table.

Dom licked the blob of custard left on his fork from the Neapolitan he'd polished off then pushed his plate away.

"That was *delizioso*, but I hate to tell Sarah it isn't a traditional Italian dessert like your pizzelle." Dom pointed to the thin waffle cookie on Claire's plate.

Claire broke off a small piece of the anisette-flavored cookie. "It's quite delicious, but I don't dare eat too much. Gotta keep my health up, you know."

"I know. I'm going to have to add a few miles to my walking regimen to work this off." He patted his belly.

"I think you worked off some extra calories when you were chasing down Donovan," Claire said.

Dom laughed. "That was quite a chase. In retrospect, I probably shouldn't have done it, but I didn't want him to get away. I guess I still have a young man's brain in an old man's body."

"Oh, I'd say you did pretty good even if you are an old man," Claire teased.

"Meow."

Porch Cat appeared from underneath a rhododendron bush and trotted over to weave figure eights around Dom's ankles.

Claire picked a morsel of lobster from her plate and held it out to the cat, who sniffed it thoroughly before taking it gently in his mouth.

"Can you believe Zambuco actually gave us credit?" Dom asked as he watched the cat eat.

"I almost fell off my chair. Do you think he was serious about having us consult on cases?"

Dom had wondered if Zambuco was serious, too. If he was, did they want to take him up on it? He sneaked a look at Claire.

In their younger days, he'd considered her somewhat of a nuisance to work with, but he had to admit that he'd come to depend on her insights into human behavior on the past two cases. Perhaps he was growing more tolerant in his old age. Either way, he knew that investigating the murder cases had added excitement to his life and he sure did hope more of them came along.

"I'm not sure if he was serious. He's not as annoying now and it looks like Jane seems to have had something to do with tempering his cantankerous personality."

"I noticed that." Claire looked disturbed. "I'm not sure what's going on there, but it can't be all bad if it makes Zambuco act nicer. And I do have to admit, working on cases again would be interesting."

"Yes, I have to agree. These past two murder investigations have really added some spice to my life." Dom realized that during the past several days, he hadn't had time to wallow in grief. Investigating had made him feel young and invigorated, useful again.

"It would be strange after all these years to officially be partners again. Sort of like old times." Claire looked at Dom out of the corner of her eye.

"Indeed." Dom found that he could not look her straight in the eye. He had never told her about the fight he'd witnessed between Sarah and Blunt and now he felt guilty about that.

Partners did not withhold information from each other, but at the time he hadn't known that they were going to become partners. He'd thought he was just keeping an eye on Claire so as to make sure Sarah got a fair shake.

Of course, it didn't make much sense to tell Claire now. What good could come of that? It would only upset her.

"I do think our skill sets complement each other very well. We always did manage to catch the killer back in the day," he ventured.

"And we always managed to work together, even though we sometimes didn't agree on each other's methods." Claire broke off another piece of pizzelle and pushed it around her plate, unable to look Dom in the eye.

She felt guilty that she still hadn't told him that she'd seen Mae and Blunt fighting that day. Of course, Mae had admitted that herself in her kitchen when she told them the real reason for the fight, but that didn't change the fact that Claire had withheld information from her partner.

Then again, she hadn't really considered him a partner when she'd withheld the information. In her mind, she had only been teaming up with him so as to keep Mae safe from being incriminated. She considered alleviating her guilt by telling him about it now, but she didn't want him to know that she hadn't trusted him with the information. It wouldn't be a good way to start their new partnership, so she decided to let it ride.

"I actually think we work together even better now.

Perhaps age has mellowed us," Dom suggested.

Claire laughed. "I think it has. I would look forward to working together again on another case and I do hope one comes up, because it gets kind of boring around here with nothing going on."

"That's true," Dom agreed. "One can only do so many puzzles or taste test so many desserts to keep busy."

"Yes. But I don't know if you can put your puzzles away just yet. After all, how many more murders can there be on this one little island?"

"Oh, I don't know about that." Dom's left eyebrow started to tingle and he reached up and smoothed it with his index finger. "I have a feeling we just might be surprised."

A Note from the Author

Thanks so much for reading, "A Crabby Killer". I hope you liked reading it as much as I loved writing it. If you did, and feel inclined to leave a review, I really would appreciate it.

This is book two of the Mooseamuck Island Cozy Mystery Series. I plan to write many more books featuring Dom and Claire. I have several other series that I write, too - you can find out more about them on my website *http://www.leighanndobbs.com*.

This book has been through many edits with several people and even some software programs, but since nothing is infallible (even the software programs), you might catch a spelling error or mistake and, if you do, I sure would appreciate it if you let me know - you can contact me at: *lee@leighanndobbs.com*.

Oh, and I love to connect with my readers, so please visit me on facebook at *http://www.facebook.com/leighanndobbsbooks*

Signup to get my newest releases at a discount: *http://www.leighanndobbs.com/newsletter*

If you want to receive a text message on your cell phone when I have a new release, text COZYMYSTERY to 88202 (sorry, this only works for US cell phones!)

About the Author

USA Today Bestselling author Leighann Dobbs has had a passion for reading since she was old enough to hold a book, but she didn't put pen to paper until much later in life. After a twenty-year career as a software engineer with a few side trips into selling antiques and making jewelry, she realized you can't make a living reading books, so she tried her hand at writing them and discovered she had a passion for that, too! She lives in New Hampshire with her husband, Bruce, their trusty Chihuahua mix, Mojo, and beautiful rescue cat, Kitty.

Find out about her latest books and how to get discounts on them by signing up at:

http://www.leighanndobbs.com/newsletter

If you want to receive a text message alert on your cell phone for new releases, text COZYMYSTERY to 88202. (Sorry, this only works for US cell phones!)

Connect with Leighann on Facebook and Twitter:

http://facebook.com/leighanndobbsbooks
http://twitter.com/leighanndobbs

Made in the USA
Middletown, DE
28 July 2015